**CLOVIS ACADEMY LEGACY
BOOK THREE**

SHADOWS IN THE DARK

BY

Ross Harringway

**Omega Press
El Paso, TX**

CLOVIS ACADEMY LEGACY: BOOK THREE

SHADOWS IN THE DARK

OMEGA PRESS

An imprint of Omega Communications Group, Inc.

For information contact:

Omega Press
5823 N. Mesa, #839
El Paso, Texas 79912

FIRST EDITION

Printed in the United States of America

OTHER BOOK BY THE SAME AUTHOR

Clovis Academy Series

Reign of Death

Forbidden Region

CHAPTER ONE

2532 the Year of Sikorsky

The Clovis Academy cadets were in mourning due to the deaths of several classmates. The previous week had been one of the most costly in the history of the Academy. One of the most popular cadet astronauts, Amir al-Nasser, had been eaten by a giant creature in the Forbidden Region while attempting to protect another cadet. Drayton Love-Easter had been murdered on Space Station Cy-7 and five other cadets, Yuri Gorski, Michel Evart, Elektra Papanikolaou, Jen Staszko and Les Gillis, were reported lost when a transport ship they had been on suffered a hull breach in space. Seven dead cadets in four days. The student body was somber based on the news. Many students wept openly when news of the deaths swept across campus. Others were moved to stunned silence.

But not all of the cadets were saddened by the news. Many of the Bragg Gang were elated that Love-Easter, Gorski, Gillis, Staszko, Evart and Papanikolaou were dead. Cadet William Bragg convened an emergency meeting of his gang at the bar called Suicide Kings. It was one of the oldest bars in Clovis City and was frequented by transport pilots from several solar systems as well as cadets that were looking for alcohol and Red Dust at a cheap price. Bragg enjoyed the bar for the dark decor that was prevalent throughout the establishment and the fact that there were no rules. Men and women danced naked on five round stages located throughout the bar and prostitution and drugs were easy to procure. Bill Bragg had expanded the membership of the gang since the graduation of former leader Francois Zerbe. Due to his efforts to add members, the Bragg Gang had just under fifty members. Even with the superior numbers, the Gorski Gang beat them repeatedly in brawls and skirmishes. With the deaths of Gorski and the others, the Bragg Gang would be able to terrorize the other cadets with little fear from the handful of Gorski members that were left alive.

Bill Bragg led toast after toast with tequila shots as they cheered the deaths of the six cadets. His younger brother, Bret, applauded as each of the names of the dead were shouted out. James Cobb, Roy Starr, two dozen of the Lipinski sisters and other gang members joined in the celebration. Cadet astronaut John Gauthier stood in the background and refused to drink to the deaths of the cadets. Even though Gorski and Evart had been rivals to him, Gauthier felt it wrong to take pleasure in the tragedy suffered by others. He stroked his razor thin mustache as he refused to drink to the morbid toasts celebrating the misery of the friends and families of the fallen. His two best friends, cadet astronauts Basil Varek and Derek Regehr were standing at the rear of the large bar, refusing to join in as well. All three men were cadet astronauts and had considered Amir al-Nasser to have been their friend. His death had a profound impact on each of them. The three were wearing dark sweats and tennis shoes, as was normal for Gauthier, Varek and Regehr when they were not in class or in one of the many training labs.

"John, you know that Bill and Bret will be really pissed off at you if they see that you are not drinking," cadet military tactician senior Reynita Calderon whispered into his ear.

Gauthier looked into her enchanting brown eyes and shook his head as another toast was announced, leading to cheers over Love-Easter's death. Her long dark hair was loose, hanging over her brown shoulders and extending all the way down her back. She was wearing a tube top and skin tight black leather pants with boots that came up just below her knees. Her emerald colored hoop ear rings accentuated here light brown eyes.

"This is so wrong, Reynita. Yes, Gorski and I had a few fist fights in the past. Yes, I took a beating from Gillis once. I know Bill hated Drayton, especially due to the little love triangle they had going on with Yesenia. But to cheer that they died? To revel in it and celebrate it? That is not in my nature. I don't care how much I disliked them, they did not deserve what happened. And you? How are you doing? Any feelings due to Gillis being among the casualties?"

With a disgusted look on her face, Reynita pushed her shot glass of tequila away from her. She looked around the room as her brothers and sister Estrellita joined in on the toasts. "I did Les wrong. I think I will always feel bad about what I did. He was the kindest man I ever dated and I screwed him over. Now that he is dead, my biggest regret is that I never had the chance to tell him how sorry I am."

Guathier put his arm over her shoulder, "Well, Regehr and Varek are not celebrating either, if it is any consolation to you. They both feel the same way I do. And don't keep beating yourself up over what happened over three years ago. You were human and Bill used you to hurt Gillis. Instead of us listening to Bill's bullshit, perhaps we should push him out as gang leader and put someone else in charge."

Reynita smiled at him and picked up her shot glass full of tequila, "You, John?"

Gauthier shook his head, "No. I was thinking of you or Basil. You are both natural leaders. Bill is just an ass. Maybe we should oust him as leader."

Reynita downed the contents in her shot glass, "Now that I will drink to. But I nominate Basil. I really don't want to be leader."

"Why don't you?"

"I would rather concentrate on studying and graduating, John. Running a gang is not how I want to spend my spare time."

Gauthier nodded and smiled in the direction of Kornelia Lipinski. She smiled back at him. They had been involved in a friends with benefits relationship for several months. Gauthier found her to be great in bed and a great conversationalist. But he had always been a man that valued his time alone and Kornelia respected that about him. Gauthier decided that he had his fill of Bill Bragg's sick celebration over the tragedy of others. He motioned with his head to indicate to Kornelia that it was time to depart the scene and go somewhere else where they could enjoy each other's company behind closed doors. Gauthier bid Reynita, Varek and Regehr farewell before pushing through the crowd toward the exit.

Kornelia Lipinski followed Gauthier, which did not go unnoticed by several of her sisters. Like Gauthier, she did not understand the morbid need to toast to the demise of Gorski and the others. Her family had been friends with Colonel Gorski for many years and she found no joy in the untimely deaths of so many talented and promising cadets. One of her older sisters, Patrycja, followed close behind her.

"Bill is a crazy man," Patrycja told her younger sister.

"I agree, but he protects us from hazing from the other cadets," Kornelia pointed out.

"Yuri, Les and the others protected the other cadets from us," Patrycja pointed out. "Are we the bad ones or were they? I don't know where my loyalties lie any longer."

Bill Bragg was screaming to the gang in his loud booming voice that the time had come to wipe out the remaining Gorski Gang members. Kornelia shook her head in disgust, "One day he is going to meet someone bigger and stronger than he is. When that day comes, I do not want to be anywhere around him."

Patrycja nodded her agreement, "When he falls it will be very ugly. Karma is a cold bitch and Bill will find out that fact one day."

With six mixed drinks in his system, Dirk Fenster had fallen asleep in his bed with Ann Harcourt lying next to him. Ann was one of his many friends with benefits that would call on him from time to time for a night of lust. Dirk preferred his relations to remain that way and he was up front with each of his lady friends in that regard. After the news regarding the tragedy of the Transport explosion Ann wanted to "comfort" the distraught Fenster. He was happy to have the company of the young desirable lady in his bed .He had lost several individuals that were his friends. In addition, Fenster had an argument with his parents the prior evening on his holo-com device. The majority of his family lived in the country called Texas Territory on old Earth. Very few of the Fenster family ventured off Earth to explore a career in outer space or another world. Dirk had been one of the more adventurous members of his family that wanted to see and experience life on other worlds. The argument between Fenster and his parents was due to the influence he had over his younger sister named Therese. According to Dirk's mother, Therese had submitted an application for acceptance with the Clovis Academy to be like her older brother. She wanted to join her older brother on planet New Edinburgh and study mechanical engineering to earn an eventual commission with the Space Command.

To Fenster's parents, the situation was unacceptable. Therese was considered the best and the brightest of the sibling group. Her place was to train to one day take control of the family business. By filing papers to attend a military academy, Therese was showing her family that the corporation was not her priority in life. To say that her parents were angry about decision was an understatement. The fact that they put the blame on Dirk's shoulders was unfair, at least as far as he was concerned.

Many years ago, Dirk's paternal uncle had left Earth to study at another Academy on another world to become an officer. His uncle had been the first to walk away from the Fenster family fortune. He admired his uncle and corresponded with through the computer satellite mail system often. As a child, Dirk loved hearing of his adventures out in deep space and his uncle's career had been an inspiration. Although his parents vehemently objected, Dirk left Earth for the Clovis Academy so that he could become an officer in the military.

The elder parents demanded that young Dirk speak with his sister and convince her to withdraw her application. He refused their demand and advocated that his parents embrace the mature choice Therese had made. That was when the expletives and the threats began. Dirk was told that his monthly allowance from the family would be cut off if he did not do as he was told. Dirk responded by telling his parents to stick their money and the fortune where the Earth's Sun would not shine. The conversation lasted only a few seconds after that ill-advised comment by Dirk.

Accordingly, Dirk had been in a depressed mood until Ann Harcourt made sexual advances at him. He took her up on her invitation and guided her to his room with the hope that making love to her would get his mind off all of the past negative events.

When Dirk had arrived at his dormitory room he looked for his roommate, Arch Frazier, and found that he was not there. He had asked many of their mutual friends and found that nobody had seen Frazier at the party. That was not like Frazier to take off and say nothing. With the room all to himself, he was able to do all kinds of things with Ann Harcourt that he probably could not have done with an audience.

When Frazier finally came home it was early in the morning. He saw that Dirk was lying naked on his bed with Ann. Their clothing was strewn about on the floor and the dressers. One of Harcourt's shoes was on Frazier's pillow on his bed. Frazier quietly lay down on his bed and softly set Harcourt's errant shoe on the floor. He stared at the ceiling deep in thought about the things he had seen in the last twenty-four hours. Frazier had paid pilot Giles Lancer to fly his private transport ship to Space Station Cy-7 so that they could bring Yuri Gorski, Les Gillis, Jen Staszko, Michel Evart and Elektra Papanikolaou safely home. Frazier had been sworn to secrecy by Colonel Gorski regarding the return of Gorski and the others and he intended to keep that secret. But Dirk was his best friend and Frazier felt that he could fully trust him. Frazier hoped that whatever Colonel Gorski had in mind, that it happened sooner rather than later. The idea of keeping a secret from Dirk, especially one involving the return of their close friends, was not a task Frazier relished. Theodora, Dirk's pet Timber Wolf, jumped on the bed with Frazier and licked his face. He pet her and scratched the large wolf behind her ears. Theodora cuddled up next to Frazier and she fell asleep.

CHAPTER TWO

Marco Andolini stirred in his dormitory room bed and looked at his holo-com device on the dresser to his left.

It was only three a.m.

He was unable to sleep due to the news of his friends dying in the transport explosion. Asleep next to him was Mary Lincoln. Marco had always found Lincoln attractive, but since she had been Yuri Gorski's girlfriend, Marco never pursued her. The unwritten rule in the Gorski Gang was that no one took another's girl or man from another gang member. Gorski demanded that his friends remain loyal to each other and that loyalty would foster respect and friendship. Months back, when Gorski and Lincoln split up, Marco never acted on his urge to date the lovely lady as the prevailing wisdom was that Yuri and Mary would get back together again. But now things were much different. After the split, Jen Staszko had been successful in her campaign to land Gorski for herself. Staszko knew a good man when she saw him and moved in after

Gorski the moment he was a free man.

After the party at the women's dormitory building began to end, Marco offered to walk Mary to her room. He found in quick time that the attraction he had for her was reciprocated by her. They both gave in to their mutual affections for one another and ended up in Marco's room and they made love for their first time. He savored the feel of her naked body against his, the smell of her perfume and the taste of her full lips. She was beautiful and a great lover. After they had sex, she was able to fall asleep. Marco could not as he knew someone or several someone's had killed his friends. Gorski had warned him of a possible cover-up in Drayton Love-Easter's murder. Marco had known Gorski for many years and he was not one to make wild accusations or come to baseless conclusions. If Gorski believed there to be a possible conspiracy, then there very well may be one.

Marco slowly slid out of bed, doing his best to not wake Lincoln. He walked quietly past his brother's bed, which was empty. Most likely Dominic was with Harumi Shigeta at her dormitory room. Marco had always been happy for his brother for finding a quality lady like Shigeta. Since the Andolini brothers were both sports stars, they had numerous women that threw themselves at them. Marco had been the promiscuous one of the Andolini brothers and generally had a different lady on his arm every weekend. Dominic had always been more reserved, shunning most of the women that stalked the pro sports athletes. Marco had slept with dozens of women over the last few years; the vast majority were soccer groupies that were always available after each game. Dominic did not get involved with the women that would throw themselves at him. Marco concluded that that Shigeta and Dominic were a good match. Both were family oriented, both were loyal to their friends and they were both smart, educated and athletic. She was a good woman and treated Dominic well.

Marco showered, shaved and brushed his teeth. He stood in silence for a few minutes, looking into the mirror as he contemplated all of the events of the last few days. His friend Amir had been killed because of that idiot McWilliams. Drayton had been murdered. Then Yuri, Michel, Les, Jen and Elektra were killed. And now, Marco had the woman of his dreams in his bed. Marco began to cry as he thought of his friends that were now lost. He and Gorski had met on the Battle Cruiser *Argonaut* when they were being transported to this new planet. They were just six years old at the time.

Children.

Over the years they had become close as brothers. For many years, Dominic, Yuri and Marco were inseparable. The Andolini and Gorski families spent all of the holidays together. They would eat dinner at each other's homes. Yuri Gorski was considered an uncle to Marco's younger siblings. They attended birthday celebrations for each other. Together, Dominic, Marco and Yuri made up the original Gorski's Gang. When Drew Harrison came along, they were sometimes called the Four Horsemen of Apocalypse. Marco laughed to himself about that and had wondered what they had done to deserve such a nickname. He also wondered which of the four he was. They had never started a fight, although they would make the folks that challenged them pay for it.

Marco walked back to his bed and noticed that Lincoln had kicked off the covers; her fantastic body was illuminated by the light of the New Edinburgh moon. He slid into the bed next to her and she stirred and rolled over into his arms. He held her and stared at the ceiling of his room. His heart was broken over the loss of his dear friends.

He heard Lincoln whisper to him, "Trouble sleeping?"

"Yes," he admitted to her.

"Then make love to me again. I want to take all of your energy from you so you can rest," Lincoln said as she began roaming her hands over his body. She had gone months without a lover after her break up with Gorski. Finding a good man was difficult for a woman in their century. The statistics indicated that there were eight to eight point six women for every male. The odds of finding and keeping a man were not good, especially since most men would elect to use their rights to take extra wives. Now that she had Marco she planned on making up for lost time and he proved that he was more than willing to oblige her.

Cadet astronaut Jack Harcourt had taken solitude on the rooftop of the main men's dormitory building. He had been one of the heroes of the day for his role in the rescue of Cadet Tina Martinson in the Forbidden Region. Several of the female cadets had shown interest in sharing his bed with him that night. But Harcourt wanted to be alone and politely refused the offers for sex he had received. He felt guilty that he had left Space

Station Cy-7 a day early as he might have been able to help his friends. Jack was a Child of Athena, with milky white skin, dark eyes and hair and mental powers that would have been useful in getting his friends to safety. He could read minds, move objects and his most powerful gift was the ability to take control of another person's mind, temporarily taking form them their free will and forcing them to do things that they would not normally do. Of all the other Gorski Gang members, Harcourt had been closest to Michel Evart. They had been dormitory roommates for three years and studied together all the time. Harcourt cherished all of the times that Evart helped him with his class work and advised him of which Professors to avoid.

Harcourt had a bottle of whiskey in his hands as he stood at the edge of the tall building, leaning his muscular arms on the metallic safety wall that came up to his chest and taking an occasional drink as he stared up at the stars. He gazed out at the skyline of dozens of skyscraper buildings that were all around the Academy. To his left was one of the tallest towers, the Rosenburg Law Firm Building, which was several kilometers from the Academy but was so large that it seemed as if it was only a few blocks away. Harcourt was able to see long distances and in the dark due to the genetic manipulation from the medical staff that had created him. He could see all around, which was one of the main reasons he sought the comfort of the rooftops of buildings and why he hoped to be a pilot. In the four years that he had lived in Clovis City, Harcourt witnessed the rapid growth as people from other planets immigrated to

New Edinburgh with the promise of land and jobs.

Harcourt thought of his friend Evart and the numerous discussions they shared regarding the immigration issue. Since Evart had been one of the immigrants, he was sensitive to the name calling from the original settlers of the planet. Evart once told Harcourt that he could not wait to graduate so that he could leave the purple planet behind. Evart had dreamed of the day that he would be out there in deep space, flying a large battle ship. Harcourt grieved that his friend never realized his dream. He took a drink and looked up at the stars in the night sky, "Good bye, my friend."

Rolf Rhinehard felt badly for the lost gang members as well. But unlike Harcourt, Rolf found solace in with three female cadets with loose morals and convinced them to engage in a foursome in his dormitory room. After he had sex with all three women, they passed out on his bed. He looked over the naked women, and realized that he had selected a diverse set. The white girl, Maria Haake, was a bit overweight but her ample breasts made up for that. The dark skinned girl, LaTania Serpas, was in amazing shape and Rolf liked bedding her the most. And then the Asian girl with the last name of Zhizhi, was slender and had amazing legs. Rolf fell asleep in the middle of the three nude women with a smile on his face. They had helped him forget his grief over the deaths for at least one evening.

Cadet astronaut Porfirio Cardenas lived in the married cadets housing area. The homes for those students were segregated from the dormitories for the single men and women to keep any children of the couples away from the sexual escapades of the single cadets. Cardenas preferred it that way, as the singles dorms tended to be loud with several parties during the week. The married couples would share the occasional cook out or soccer game in the field behind their subdivision. Like the rest of the married couples, Cardenas liked the peace and quiet as well as the privacy of his own home.

He watched with sadness the prior evening when Admiral Seward delivered the news of Amir al-Nasser's death to his three wives. The al-Nasser family lived across the cul-de-sac from Cardenas and they had become good friends over the past three years. Cardenas heard the wails of despair from one of the wives as Seward told them that their husband was dead. He silently prayed to God to watch over the women and their children during their time of hardship.

Cardenas and his wife, Freya Doernitz, had met when she was just eighteen years old. She had been sent by her adopted family, the Yamamoto's, to attend the Academy in Clovis City. Freya already had one year in the Academy when Cardenas started his first year. They were immediately drawn to each other, he being the young, handsome student pilot and she the attractive medical student. Their whirlwind relationship produced a marriage within a few months and two children in rapid succession. Their children were Alejandro Doernitz Cardenas, age three and Maria Yamamoto Cardenas, age two. Freya had graduated near the top of her class and served as a Doctor at the Cordell Hull United Nations

Hospital in the Clovis City Province. The hospital was just one kilometer away from the main United Nations Tower and the New Edinburgh Administrative Buildings. Freya held the rank of Army First Lieutenant in the Medical Service Corps. Her uniform was the one piece light blue medical outfit that was standard issue at her hospital. She worked in the emergency ward as all new incoming doctors had to do as part of their learning process. Completing medical training was a challenge given Freya had given birth to two children while in the Academy. Part of the reason she made it through was the support of her husband, Porfirio and in part due to her little brother, Jurgen, who had followed her to New Edinburgh a year and a half ago.

Jurgen Doernitz also joined the Academy due to the influence of their adopted family. The Academy normally did not allow single cadets to live in the married cadet housing, but the administration made an exception for Jurgen due to Admiral Yamamoto's requests. Jurgen gladly helped with his nephew and niece whenever he was not in class or at the simulator training rooms. He lived in one of the spare bedrooms in the home and the two children each had their own room. The homes for the married cadets were roomy, with large kitchens and spacious dining area. To assist the married cadets with finances, each home came fully stocked with furniture, appliances and beds.

Jurgen Doernitz was always home early, so his sister Freya was surprised when she woke up at five a.m. and heard her son, Alejandro, asking for his uncle.

"Mama, en donde es mi tio?" Alejandro asked Freya as she was brushing her long blonde hair.

"In German," Freya told her son. She and her husband had determined that they would teach their children at least three languages before they started their first year of public schooling. The three year old boy scratched is head, thinking.

"Wo ist meine..." Alejandro paused, thinking and scratching the back of his head. "Meine Lieblingsonkel?"

Freya smiled at him, "Very good! Now, in English?"

"Where is my uncle?" Alejandro asked.

Freya hugged her son, "Very good. I am so proud of you. Let's go see where uncle Jurgen is, okay?" She picked him up in her arms and carried him to the bedroom where Uncle Jurgen slept. She opened the door and saw that the bed was empty.

Freya frowned and carried her son back to her bedroom. Her husband was in the shower. She knocked on the bathroom door and spoke loud enough for him to hear over the running water. "My love, Jurgen is not here. Did you see him leave this morning?"

Cardenas came out of the large walk in shower with a towel around his waist, "What happened honey? Did you say that Jurgen is not home?"

"No, his bed looks like it was never slept in," Freya told him. She kissed her husband on the cheek. Porfirio kissed his son on the cheek as well.   "Guten Morgen, Vater," Alejandro greeted him.

"Very good, baby," Freya said as she sat Alejandro back on the ground. "Go help your sister get ready for Day Care."

Alejandro ran off yelling, "Maria! Wake up!"

Freya put her arms around Porfirio's shoulders and kissed him. "So, husband, where is my little brother?"

"Well, I told you last night about what happened with Amir," Cardenas said as he began dressing into his cadet flight uniform. "Your little brother became a hero overnight."

"As did you."

"Yes, well, not like Jurgen," he told her as he grabbed his black boots from the walk-in closet. "He caught the eye of several of the girls and gained immediate respect from Marco. They invited him over to one of their infamous cook outs at the women's dormitory."

"What? Wait a minute Mister Family Values!" Freya shook her finger playfully at him. "Are you saying that you, you of all people, allowed my little brother, your brother-in-law, to go off to a party with scantily clad sexy dormitory women under the direction of playboy Marco Andolini?"

Cardenas was forcing on his left boot. "Yes I did," he said proudly.

"Really?" She was in disbelief. "And I suppose the fact he did not return means one of those scantily clad women took advantage of my kid brother?"

Cardenas laughed, "Well there were two, Cara Guerrero and Melissa Harcourt, who were certainly giving Jurgen the eye. They both seemed very interested."

Freya grabbed her shoulder bag on the bedroom dresser which was full of food packets for Maria and Alejandro to eat at their day care center. "So, if my brother breeds with one of those DNA spliced Harcourt girls, I will have you to blame?"

"DNA spliced Harcourt girls?" Cardenas was laughing as he finished putting on his second boot. "Come on, Melissa is a nice girl. I have no doubt she will be good to Jurgen. I am not sure which of the two would have been bold enough to make a move on him, but I could see that he also likes them both."

"So, my little brother lost his virginity last night?" Freya said thoughtfully. Her brother had never really shown any interest in pursuing a girlfriend. He was always learning battle patterns, flight techniques, studying on his three dimensional displays, all to become the best pilot he could be. Freya had always hoped some pretty girl would take interest in Jurgen and make a move on him. Jurgen was always so deep into his studies that he seemed to not even notice women.

"Knowing Cara and Melissa, the way they both talk about their sexual conquests, I would say there was a high statistical probability that one of them was going to make advances on your brother's chastity." Cardenas stood up.

"Yes!" Freya said as if she were celebrating a great event. "My little brother finally got laid!"

"And that is something to celebrate?"

She kissed her husband, "Gotta get the kids to day care. See you tonight. And stay away from those scantily clad Academy girls!"

"You were a scantily clad Academy girl," Cardenas was laughing as he reminded her.

"And I got your attention, didn't I?" Freya said as she picked up little Maria in her right arm and took Alejandro's hand in her left.

Cardenas heard the door open and slide shut as she left the house. He called out to her, "You still have my attention!"

Jurgen Doernitz woke up to the red orange haze of the sun coming through the window of Melissa Harcourt's dormitory room. He rubbed his eyes and rolled over to his right to see that she was already awake and smiling at him. "Good morning," he told her.

"You are still here?" She asked him.

"Why would I not still be here?" He asked her as if he was confused by the question.

Melissa stretched and noticed Doernitz was gazing at her naked body. "Because most men never stick around for the morning."

Doernitz frowned, thinking how wonderful her body was. "That's crazy. I could stay here all day just, just watching you. I feel like this is the only place worth being in the morning."

Melissa smiled at that. "You are so sweet," she said as she sat up and leaned over Doernitz and gave him a long lingering kiss. She rolled on top of him and began kissing him passionately. Doernitz responded. They made love under the glare of the rising sun through her windows. Doernitz never dreamed that having a girlfriend could be so pleasurable.

CHAPTER THREE

As a career military officer, he was used to being contacted before sunrise to go to clandestine meetings to discuss random events or issues that had come up. The call from Major Evart did not startle retired Admiral Seward at all. He agreed to meet the Major and quickly dressed, wondering what was so critical that it required the presence of a cadet pilot instructor at the United Nations Building. He speculated that it was possibly some routine meeting regarding a background check of some random cadet that had gotten into trouble the previous evening. But he was about to find that the reason he was losing sleep that morning was something he had never encountered before.

Retired Admiral Seward was escorted to one of the sound proof meeting rooms in one of the underground bunkers of the United Nations Tower by two Marine Corps enlisted men in their dress blues. Seward had to clear metal detector, lithium and radiation security scans and identity confirmations by producing his finger and palm prints on a computer screen. Once Seward had been cleared, he entered the building and then took an elevator ride down about twenty floors down to reach the bunkers.

The underground bunkers had been created by architects and engineers decades ago so that the higher ranking government employees would have a place for safety in the event of an alien attack. They were built on New Edinburgh by the Brackenridge family construction business. Many secret deals and negotiations were rumored to have occurred in bunkers on all of the planets occupied by the United Nations of Earth. Seward had never been invited to such a clandestine meeting in the underground section until that day. In military service, the time to report to duty was considered paramount. Promptness was taught religiously to every enlisted soldier, non-commissioned officer and officer in the Space Command. Be on time, or else. Even though Seward was retired, old habits die hard.

Seward entered a large conference hall that resembled what seemed to be a Restaurant Mess Hall for the individuals that would be stuck in the bunker in time of war. But today at four thirty in the morning, there was a small handful of people present sitting at the tables. Seward stopped in his tracks when he saw them.

"You're supposed to be dead," Seward said with astonishment.

Cadet Yuri Gorski stood up when he saw the Admiral. Michel Evart did as well. Jen Staszko, Elektra Papanikolaou and Les Gillis were asleep, resting their heads on the tables.

"Good morning Admiral," Yuri Gorski told him. "My father should be here soon. We have some things to discuss."

"Yes, yes we do," Seward said, sitting down at one of the tables. He was bewildered that the news reports regarding the five cadets before him were wrong. He was obviously glad that they were alive, but their presence was most likely the reason he was summoned so early in the morning. "I am glad the five of you are alive. Everyone at the Academy was saddened when we got the news reports that you were dead. What exactly is going on here?"

"We think there might be someone out there wanting to kill us," Evart said softly, not wanting to wake their three sleeping friends.

"And why would they want to kill you?" Seward was curious.

"Because we witnessed the murder of our friend Drayton and there is someone big covering it up. The fact that the transport that we were supposed to be on blew up proves that they were out to get us," Gorski explained. He noticed that Seward looked about as tired as he felt. "We made some coffee, Admiral. Would you like some?"

Seward nodded in the affirmative, "Thanks. Coffee right now would be great."

The entire roster of professors and instructors at the Clovis Academy had been informed that the five cadets sitting before Seward died in the explosion. Seward liked Gorski and Evart, as he had the pleasure of teaching them flight techniques. The other three cadets were not training to be pilots, so Seward had little to no contact with them at all. The fact these two promising young men were still living was fantastic news to Seward. The Space Command needed good pilots and Evart and

Gorski were steady hands with the talent to be good flight officers. Seward could see the exhaustion in the eyes of Evart and Gorski. Seward surmised that the two cadets had not slept at all in over twenty-four hours.

They heard the doors to the Hall open and the three turned to see Colonel Gorski, Major Evart, Clovis Academy Dean Golden Harvard and attorney Sean Collins walk into the room. Both Gorski and Evart were in their camouflage uniforms while Collins was wearing a dark grey business suit and Harvard was in a blue and white one piece pull over with blue slippers on his feet. Harvard had not been used to waking up so early in the morning so he threw on the easiest outfit possible. His grey hair was uncombed and his eyes looked bloodshot.

Yuri Gorski was pouring coffee for Seward when he saw the Dean of the University walk in with his father. Gorski swallowed hard as Dean Harvard never got personally involved in issues regarding students unless it was something serious. In those rare events, the cadets involved found that Harvard was a strict disciplinarian. Many cadets were suspended or kicked out of the Academy when they were brought to Harvard's attention.

Golden Harvard was sixty years old, tall, with grey hair. He was skinny, not a man that would be able to find his way around a gymnasium, but he was a respected writer and researcher of history and warfare. Harvard had published dozens of articles and several books on past battles. He was considered one of the most effective writers at breaking down the strategy and execution of each side in the past conflicts. He would even write about how the outcome of certain battles may have turned out differently, had the losing commanders been less brain dead. Harvard had several wives, many children and even more grandchildren. Harvard and his wives used special drugs that were recommended by the Glorious Leader for increased fertility. With the assistance of the drugs, Harvard's sperm count increased dramatically and his wives were able to produce many more eggs than normal. The result was more pregnancies with twins, triplets or more. The only side effect of the drug was that the chance of having a girl as opposed to a boy was ten to one in favor of a girl.

Sean Collins was the chief attorney for the United Nations Security Council on New Edinburgh. He was well known for his skills as a trial lawyer and had a reputation as a tireless worker. He could quote rules of evidence, statutes, treaties and appeals court opinions by memory. He was in good shape and enjoyed competing in forty-two kilometer marathon runs to keep himself fit.

Collins had several children as well, but nowhere near the numbers in the Harvard household. Only four of his children, Ginger, Siobhan, Liam and Sean, III, had attended the Academy on Clovis. His other children were too young to enter the collegiate level. Siobhan was a graduating senior and was studying Life Sciences and was planning on becoming a doctor. Yuri knew her well because she had been his "friend with benefits" before he met Mary Lincoln.

Ginger Collins O'Grady had married another graduating cadet doctorate candidate named Eamon O'Grady. Ginger was one of those gifted people that was a master at operating computer systems with little effort. She worked at the United Nations Tower as a Computer Technician in the civilian service. One year at the Annual War Games competition Ginger finished in first place, beating out over two thousand contestants. It was a contest in which the participants would play against each other using the newest three dimensional holographic computer technology games. If one was in a battle and needed one person to operate the computer defense systems, Ginger would be the one to select.

Sean Collins, III, also known by his middle name Cormac, was a nineteen year old student at the Academy studying weapons and mechanical engineering. Gorski had little to no interaction with the student as he seemed to keep to himself. Les Gillis, on the other hand. spent some of his spare time interacting with the Collins children as they were regulars at O'Malley's and would sing old Irish ballads together.

The fourth Collins offspring that Gorski knew of was Liam. He was a quiet eighteen years old and seemed to enjoy the study of animals, especially dinosaurs. Liam also was generally fairly quiet and reserved. Liam would normally accompany his siblings to some of the bars and restaurants in Clovis City and would not have much to say. All four of the Collins children were considered good kids by the other families in the community. Gorski knew there were other children of the Collins clan, but he had never met them.

"Let's all sit together," Sean Collins suggested to the group. "Yuri, make more coffee. I think some are not used to going all night without sleep."

Yuri nodded and began to prep another pot of coffee. He was not surprised that Collins would remember him. Several years ago, Collins had caught Yuri having sex with his daughter Siobhan at his mansion home. Yuri had to run from the angry father, leaving all of his clothes behind as he made his way back to the men's dormitory which was a mile away. Fortunately it was a school night and not many cadets saw the naked Gorski running across campus. Of course, that had happened almost four years ago. What attorney Collins did not know was that Gorski and Siobhan had been sexually active together for two years before he had caught them.

Gorski brought several cups of coffee over and served the participants. Michel Evart helped Gorski. Everyone found seats and were soon sitting together at one of the round tables.

"So," Collins began, breaking the silence in the room, "Colonel Gorski asked me to explore the legality of what he is about to request of the Academy. I need to disclose that I work for the United Nations Security Council. That is my client. If Dean Harvard here needs legal counsel, then he will have to hire his own. Does everyone understand?" He waited a moment as everyone nodded their heads. Collins had wanted to make certain that none of the parties present would later make claims that he was their lawyer. The Rules of Professional Responsibility were strict on the issues of the formation of an attorney-client relationship. Collins always practiced with caution in that area, setting out the parameters of the professional connection up front.   "Good. Colonel

Gorski and Major Evart wish to station five soldiers from the branches of Military Intelligence or Marines as undercover agents at the Academy. These Marines and MI are to be given fake enrollment papers to the college, attend classes as students and live in the dormitories. They will act as students in every manner except that they are primarily going to be working as personal body guards to the five cadets here in this bunker."

Collins paused and sipped the coffee given to him. "Tastes terrible, but keep it coming." Everyone that worked with Collins knew that he would drink three to six cups of coffee daily. He was always a fast paced person, wanting things done immediately. "Legally, the Clovis Academy has a ban on weapons on campus facilities such as hand lasers and laser rifles. If these Marines are enrolled to pose as students the question is, can they have concealed weapons? I believe that they may."

"Why is that?" Harvard spoke up. The Dean hated weapons, saw no reason for them and had expelled students in the past for carrying such weapons. He felt they had no place on his campus unless for training purposes.

"Well, I found no statutory laws or appellate case law on point here on New Edinburgh," Collins told them. "So, I researched the other planets under the United Nations of the Eight Solar Systems for any guidance. I found an appeals decision written by the Martian Colonies Supreme Court from twenty-eight years ago. The case was styled Frye versus United Nations Space Command. The case involved a serial killer stalking and murdering female cadets on the Martian Colony Academy. The criminal investigation division sent in some undercover officers to pose as students. They all carried their hand lasers, concealed as they played 'student' and let themselves be easy targets for the stalker. The killer, Frye, attacked one of the female CID undercover operatives and she blasted him with her hand laser. He died and his parents sued for monetary damages under the theory the CID agents were students and the law prohibited the weapons on campus and that law was narrowly tailored to avoid such a death on campus. The Supreme Court on Mars in an en banc opinion stated that the CID agents were operating in a sanctioned undercover operation to protect the student population from a known threat, Frye, and therefore were really law enforcement and not students. No damages were awarded to the family."

"So, then, our plan is legally okay?" Major Evart asked.

"In my opinion, yes," Collins told them. "Law enforcement has a duty to protect the innocent. Therefore, officers of the law can carry weapons, even if they are 'acting' like a student. But, the opinion is specific to law enforcement. I found no opinions addressing Marines or MI working in an undercover operation."

Harvard grunted. His arms were crossed in front of his chest. "So, you gentlemen want me to authorize five undercover soldiers to act like students on my campus to protect these five cadets from the possibility of an attack?"

"Yes, Dean Harvard, that is exactly what I wish for you to do," Colonel Gorski responded.

Harvard took a large gulp from his coffee cup and he looked over at Collins. "You are right. This coffee tastes like Poggie crap. All right, I will reluctantly authorize this. But make sure you select five reliable men and women. I do not want any students getting caught in a cross fire because you put some reckless cowboy on my campus."

"We will hand pick them ourselves," Colonel Gorski assured him. "And it will be three men and two women."

"Send them to see me at the campus offices," Harvard instructed as he stood up. The Dean did not like the idea, but if it meant protecting the five cadets, he was willing to agree to anything reasonable. "I will get them enrolled and situated personally."

"Thank you for cooperating, sir," Major Evart shook Harvard's hand.

Colonel Gorski stood up and handed Harvard a round computer memory diskette. "We have all of the information that you will need for the five undercover agents on this disk. If you can get them entered into your system before lunch time that would be appreciated."

"I will get it done," Harvard said, sticking the disk in his pocket. "When do these five cadets come back to resume class? The students all believe them dead. When they show back up, it will cause quite a stir."

"Immediately," Colonel Gorski told him as he glared in the direction of Yuri. "My son has missed too much class already."

Harvard, seemingly satisfied with the answer, left the room without further comment to go back to his office.

Colonel Gorski motioned to the three sleeping cadets, "Wake them up. We need to explain the ground rules to everyone."

Yuri Gorski and Michel Evart woke their three fellow students up. They all three took a cup of coffee as they sat down with Collins, the two Marine officers and Seward.

Major Evart started the discussion, "You five will each have a shadow. We are planting three male undercover operatives and two female to act as cadets. They will be in your classes. We will get them as close to your dorm rooms as possible. Les, since you are living alone, we will put your guard in as your room mate."

Gillis made a face when he tasted the coffee, "Who made this stuff? Make sure my shadow is not allergic to cats."

"Why?" Major Evart asked. "Do you have a Kotek girlfriend or something?"

"No, I have a domestic cat, I should say Drayton did. But I will care for him," Gillis said. "So, we will each be shadowed. What are our restrictions? Do we have a curfew?"

"No," Colonel Gorski was pacing as he talked. "I want all five of you to live normally so anyone observing will believe we are not on to them. Don't even think about your guards as soldiers. They will be students, as each of you are, and will be in your classes and follow you everywhere. For this to work, they need to be a part of your gang. Just bring all five of them into your inner circle so they can always be around or nearby. Tell everyone that you met them on the space station and that they were transferring cadets and you all got to know each other. Make up something plausible so the other students do not question their presence."

"When do we go back to class?" Staszko asked. She also thought the coffee was atrocious. But she bit her tongue on the issue as her lover, Yuri Gorski, had always deluded himself into believing his coffee was great tasting. Out of fear of insulting the Colonel, she did not voice her opinion that having the shadows would not be necessary. In her opinion, she and the others were perfectly capable of fending for themselves.

"Right now," Seward told them. "I will personally take you back to the dormitory rooms. Your shadows will be in place by noon."

"Secrecy is key," Major Evart stressed.

Everyone nodded that they were in agreement of what was going to happen. Yuri Gorski felt he should tell his father about Gillis and Penelope Smith, but that could wait until things started happening. Gorski knew he could not reveal to his father that they had purchased stun darts and other items from Giles Lancer the night before. If anything bad happened, his father would find out soon enough. Most important to Yuri was that his father could have the ability to claim ignorance and deny knowledge that the cadets carried illegal weapons.

"I am going to take my son outside for a moment," Colonel Gorski announced to the group. "Yuri, come with me."

Yuri Gorski followed his father to the entrance of the Hall and out the sliding doors. Colonel Gorski waited for his son in the hallway. The door to the Hall slid shut.

"Son, what have I told you about getting into trouble?" Colonel Gorski hissed as he punched his son in the chest.

"Dad, we did not go looking for trouble!" The younger Gorski protested. "Those guys were there to hurt Elektra. Dray got in their way! They killed him. We were not looking for trouble, dad. I swear it. We were in our hotel rooms and these men attacked."

Colonel Gorski paced back and forth in front of his son, listening to his explanation. "Son, you have the chance to have a fantastic career in the Space Command. I was proud of you when you graduated Spetsnaz. So was Piotr. Your mother would have been proud, too. You will be one of the elite officers after you graduate because you went through that specialized training. If you graduate, that is."

"I will dad. I promise that I will graduate."

"Yuri, trouble seems to find you and your friends everywhere you go. It took four years for one of your group to get killed, which is surprising given all the shenanigans you have gotten into." Colonel Gorski paused and glared at his son. "These other cadets in your group respect and admire you. They see in you a natural born leader. Live up to their expectations of you. Humans do not give their loyalty to others easily. These kids all trust you. I can see it in their eyes that they would all follow you to hell and back."

"I know that dad," Yuri looked at the door, thinking of his friends in the other room. "And I always have done my best to watch out for all of them."

"And now one is dead!" Colonel Gorski pointed at his son. "Now, this is how it will be from this day and each day until graduation. The man I assign to be your shadow will become your new best friend. You will do as he says at all times. Understand?"

"Yes father."

"Yuri, these people that you saw have means and connections. They killed all those people on that transport ship, as you have speculated, which would suggest they are immoral and dangerous." Colonel Gorski sighed, "It is almost as if we are reliving Dark October all over again. Whoever these people are, they have proven to be lethal and committed to one thing and that is killing you and your friends. They have high tech weaponry and seem to have no concern for the lives of others."

"I know."

"Then, if there really is a conspiracy going on here, make sure that we catch those bastards soon. They will come for you and your four friends in there," Colonel Gorski pointed to the Restaurant Hall doorway. "Make certain that you keep everyone together. When they come, and they will, you need to be ready. Son, it will be a kill or be killed situation."

"Yes father," Yuri nodded.

"And always remember that your little brother idolizes you. He watches everything that you do and will mimic your actions. Remember that. Keep Piotr out of this." Colonel Gorski motioned for the doorway to the Hall, signaling that the conversation was over with as far as he was concerned.

The five students departed for the Academy Dormitories with retired Admiral Seward, leaving behind the lawyer and the two Marine Corps officers drinking the bad tasting coffee. They sat in silence for a moment, to make sure no one was coming back.

Collins broke the absence of sound, "So, does either of the two of you really believe that there is some cover up going on in the Love-Easter murder?"

Colonel Gorski was pacing again, "My son may be a carouser, a womanizer and he may drink a little at parties. But he has never lied to me. If he says he saw more than one killer then I believe him. The fact his four friends say the same thing only corroborates the story."

"As well as some of the witness statements at the hotel fifth floor on the night in question," Major Evart added. He had read some of the reports of Lieutenant Garrison and recalled that the customers claimed that there were several combatants involved that night. "And with the head of space station security dead, who knows what this is all about or who would be involved?"

Collins nodded thoughtfully, "I have tried many cases, both before the Judge and juries. I will tell you that conspiracies do happen. Cover ups do happen. Dark October was a cover up and we each lost people we cared about in that attack. The human psyche knows no bounds when it comes to viciousness and depravity. All five cadets told us the same story which suggests to me that they are credible. I believe these kids. I studied the disk for the investigation all morning. There is something rotten going on at the Baroness Hotel."

"Agreed," Gorski muttered as he sat down. "Now, the question is do we bring in Secretary General Lyss on this one? He might have some insight into who would have the influence, money and power to cover this up."

Collins leaned back in his chair and exhaled loudly, "I can name on my ten fingers who would have such money and power to do this. That would be the major land owners of the ten Provinces not named Clovis City."

"The Lynotts, the Rosenburgs, the Nours, the Kanders, the Wards and Essex family," Major Evart recited the surnames of some of the most powerful families on the planet.

"Yes, those are some tantalizing names," Collins tapped his fingers on the table. "And each of them has the resources to do things under the table. The question is which one of the ten most powerful families on New Edinburgh did this?"

"How do we find out?" Gorski wanted to know. "We send in CID asking questions, it will tip them off. We send in spies, they run the risk of being the next victim."

"The key is that we have to be patient," Collins said thoughtfully. "All criminals make mistakes. I suspect these criminals have already made some errors. Mistake number one was the man that supposedly confessed to the murder. I pulled up pictures of the man. He was fatter than any man I have ever seen. I do not believe that someone that out of shape can singlehandedly best a twenty year old man that is in fantastic physical conditioning and a Spetsnaz graduate. They killed this Khartov to keep him quiet."

"Who killed him?" Major Evart demanded.

"His own lawyer killed him," Collins stood up and downed the last gulp of coffee. "Check into an Ellis Ragnarsson. He is a law partner with Alfred Rosenburg, III. Their law office is located right here in Clovis City in the tallest tower in the city. In fact, Rosenburg owns the building and leases out the other floors to some fairly well off businesses. Put some pressure on Ellis Ragnarsson and see what he says."

"Do you know this Ellis Ragnarsson?" Gorski asked.

"No, never met him personally," Collins told the officers. "I checked the case listings in the U.N. building and that lawyer generally only handles criminal law. Some assaults, theft, many drug cases and treason cases. He seems to get his clients to plea out and take deals as opposed to going to trial. That is all I know right now but I will dig some more. I also recommend that you have some people look into the employees at the Baroness Hotel. Malfunctions on security equipment at the precise time a crime is being committed is never an accident. It was intentional. You gentlemen need to get me information on the identifies of each and every employee at that establishment. So, the Hotel and Ragnarsson. Get your local CID to jump on those two leads. The more we can investigate on the planetary surface the more we can lull the culprits on Cy-7 into believing that we have bought their bull crap story."

Collins then politely excused himself and left the two Marines to do their jobs. Collins found his own way out of the underground bunkers and began walking toward his offices in the United Nations Administration Building. With all of the current events and intrigue, it was going to be a long and stressful week.

After he had left the room, Evart turned to Gorski. "Ever since his wife died he seems more high strung, wouldn't you agree?"

"Yes, he has always been an excellent lawyer but I have noticed his bouts with insomnia and then his extended sick leave. I always wonder where Sean goes off to when he is not working. Just be glad he is with us and on our side. He is one of the best lawyers on the planet and he did just give us the direction that we need to go in to properly investigate my son's claims. The cafeteria should be opening about now and I already informed Mark Lund to meet us there so that I could brief him on the situation. Let's go get some real coffee," Gorski suggested.

CHAPTER FOUR

Achilles Academy on Sikorsky's Planet was in full swing as students, faculty and other employees rushed all over the vast campus of ninety-three lecture buildings and thirty astronaut simulation training complexes were available for the masses. With just under 75,000 cadets it was one of the largest military Academy's in the Eight Solar Systems. The students were a good mixture of the population of the planet. The student body consisted of about ninety percent humans. The other ten percent consisted of Kotek's, the half human and half feline hybrids, a few Harcourt's, some Falcon's which were hybrid human and bird beings and even some of the native Akarzdamedians had enrolled as students.

Caine Rosenburg was beginning his senior year at Achilles Academy. When he wasn't stalking some unlucky girl for his lust for rape, torture and murder, he would spend his time studying weapons and military history. In his last year, Caine had failed two history courses. His father paid the Dean of the University to change the grades. Caine's two failing grades were reviewed by the Dean and changed to the passing grades of "B."

Caine had his injured arm in a sling. On two occasions he bumped his arm against a wall which caused him some discomfort and reminded him of the Clovis Academy cadets that had hurt him. He was satisfied that his family had gotten revenge on them all. After all, he was a Rosenburg and those cadets existed for his pleasure. They had no right to stand up to him and his friends. His cover story at the campus was that he had been injured in a hunting accident. None of the Professors dared questioned Caine as to where he had been the days he missed. The word had trickled down from the Dean to the Academy staff: Caine Rosenburg was untouchable. Just give him a passing grade and let it go.

Caine had learned the good news that all of the people that could finger him for the murder on Space Station Cy-7 were dead. That knowledge just made Caine's day better. He walked with a purpose and was free of the cloud that had been over his head. Caine reported for his weapons training class on time and scanned the large auditorium style lecture hall. He spotted several single girls that were using three dimensional computer screens, preparing to type in notes of the lecture. In Caine's mind, each of the women was a potential target. He saw a lovely brunette sitting alone on the far side of the room and quickly decided that he wanted to have her. He found a seat behind the girl and sat down, looking over her shoulder to get a clue as to her name. If she lived in the dormitories then he would be able to stalk her easily. Caine was elated to learn that the two hour instruction of the day was the proper usage of the flame darts. The lecture hall had about two hundred students sitting in chairs facing the stage where the professor was speaking.   There was easily another three hundred seats empty. The chairs were made of dark wood found in plentiful amounts on Sikorsky's Planet. The walls were painted light blue to match the carpeting. The aisles were ramps that were on each side of the lecture hall and sloped down at about a seven percent angle.

Caine listened to his professor lecture on and on about the history of the weapon while he would look over the shoulder of the unsuspecting brunette sitting in front of him. Caine stopped listening to the teacher and looked around the lecture hall. He saw on the other side of the room Avery Jackson and Kai Chin. He nodded to the men and motioned for them to meet him after class. Jackson had his arm in a cast due to his face to face combat with Yuri Gorski. Jackson was livid that someone else had killed Gorski and he had let Caine know about his feelings. In order to cover up for the real reason Jackson had a broken arm, Caine concocted a story that Jackson had been hit by a runaway transport ship.

Caine perked up as his professor was getting to the meat of the lecture which was how to use the weapon and how the weapon kills.

"Now, what you do is this," the short, fat, bald sixty-one year old professor was stating, "you can get in close to your opponent and stab the dart into their body. You can stab their leg, arm, doesn't matter. Or, you can use the dart gun and shoot your opponent and let the weapon do the work. Now, when the dart makes contact, it automatically activates. So, if you stab an opponent, get back immediately because the dart will first eject a hard plastic barrier. If you are still touching the dart or your opponent, you might become enveloped in the barrier. Once the barrier encircles the victim, the flame dart ignites. Anything inside the plastic barrier will be incinerated by flames reaching twelve hundred degrees Fahrenheit."

The professor had a dart in his hand and had the computer cameras photograph it and enlarge the image on the wall behind him. "Now, we shall bring in a demonstration."

Caine, Jackson, Chin and the rest of the students watched as a man of Asian descent was dragged into the classroom by two guards. The man was bound by plastic arm and leg ties. He was screaming for mercy, even falling on his knees before the Professor, claiming in some language that Caine did not understand that he was innocent of the charges against him.

"This man was convicted of treason against the Glorious Leader and sentenced to death," the Professor announced to the class, ignoring the pleas of the condemned man. "His last appeal to the Supreme Court of Sikorsky's Planet was denied. Would anyone volunteer to carry out the death sentence?"

Jackson, Caine and a few others were raising their hands. The professor selected Caine, who ran down the right aisle as fast as his legs could carry him. The professor asked Caine if he knew to back away once he stabbed the man.

"Give me the damn weapon," Caine said, snatching it out of the hands of the lecturer. The prisoner was crying out, begging for his life. He kept repeating in his native tongue the word "Please" and phrases such as: "Don't do this to me."

Caine stood in silence, looking at the man, examining his face. Caine could see the tears running down his face as he continued to beg for his life. Caine took the dart into his right hand, holding it in his fist. It was shaped like a ten inch pencil. Without comment, Caine stabbed the dart into the prisoner's left shoulder and stood back. The man was screaming for mercy as the class observed a transparent bubble appear and create a round ball around the man. Two seconds after the ball formed, the pen ignited. The flames roasted the man to death as he screamed. His skin and internal organs burned into dust in seconds.

Caine smiled and walked back to his seat. He did not feel any heat from the weapon even though he had been standing just a few feet away when the flames ignited. The protective bubble was a great invention. Caine was proud of the fact that his family had created it.

When the class was finished, Caine walked out of the lecture hall, studying the direction that the pretty brunette took to her next class. He made a mental note to himself of the room number that she entered for her next class. Caine then waited in the common area of the large fifteenth floor of the University Building, crossing his arms and pacing impatiently. Avery Jackson and Kai Chin finally walked out of the class to meet him. They shook hands with Caine.

"I have news," Caine told the two men. "They were able to kill all of the witnesses and they forced a fat slob to confess to the killing of that cadet."

"That is good news," Chin was relieved.

"I already heard about it. What about the bastard that broke my arm? I told you that I wanted him for myself." Jackson was whispering due to the hundreds of Academy students walking by.

"He is dead too. I am sorry, Big Bad. But he could not be allowed to live," Caine informed him. "But you already knew that."

"I told you I wanted him for myself," Jackson snarled.

"Hey, I can't control how my family works," Caine held his hands defensively to get the giant of a man to calm down.

"That little bastard hurt me," Jackson was seething with anger. "I made it clear, he was mine. I am not happy at all about this. You tell your family that they owe me. Gorski was mine. You tell them."

Caine watched as Jackson walked away from them, "I think he is pissed."

"What was your first clue?" Chin asked as he followed after Jackson. The debacle at Space Station Cy-7 should never have happened and Chin mostly blamed Caine for the events. He had no desire to listen to whatever Caine wanted to speak to them about which was why Chin chose to follow Jackson. Chin had also been injured in the fight. He had stitches on his skull from where Love-Easter had hit him and a healing knife wound as well. Had Caine listened to anyone, they would have found an easier woman to kill and none of them would have gotten hurt and Darryl

Rosenburg would still be alive.

Caine was angered by the way the two men dismissed him. He was a member of the Royal Family and should be treated with respect. To unleash his anger, Caine spent the rest of the morning tracking the lovely brunette that he had sat behind in class. That night, he gained access to her room and he sliced her skin from her body after beating and raping her. He felt much better. He cut out her eyeballs with a specialized instrument so that he could save them for future remembrance. He left her mutilated corpse in her room as he returned to his quarters.

Clovis Academy was peaceful the next morning. The climate was bearable at eighty degrees Fahrenheit. There was a cool breeze that brought in fresh air to the city. Dean Golden Harvard had previously ordered that all of the flags be at half-mast to honor Yuri Gorski, Les Gillis, Elektra Papanikolaou, Michel Evart, Jen Staszko, Drayton Love-Easter and Amir al-Nasser. Harvard had sent out a broadcast to all of the cadets encouraging them to see grief counselors and or clergy representatives to help them all through the loss of their fellow students.

Love-Easter's body had been buried at the Clovis Academy graveyard as his father had refused to accept the corpse of his disgraced son. Amir al-Nasser had been devoured, so his three wives ordered a head stone for the military burial to honor him. Admiral Seward had visited al-Nasser's three wives the night before to inform them of their loss. They were all stunned by the death of their husband.

Both of the young men gave their lives trying to protect others.

Their deaths left a wound in the hearts of all that knew them.

Off in the distance, about fifty kilometers away, there was a brewing sand storm. The planetary climatologists were concerned as the vicious storms had a nasty habit of changing direction without warning. The scientists were monitoring the storm with keen interest and placed the entire Northern Continent on a weather alert. The Academy was put on notice that the buildings may have to go into "Lock Down" mode if the sand storm got too close. Lock Down meant all humans and animals were to be in doors until the status was lifted. The past New Edinburgh Sand Storms, although rare in occurrence, had proven deadly to life. The purple sands of the planet were coarse and if they achieved the necessary speed the sand could tear flesh and even cause rips into enviro-suits. All of the buildings on New Edinburgh had protective metal sliding doors that would cover the entire structure to protect the glass, wood and lesser metals or plastics. When the metal security doors slid down from the roofs of the buildings and secured themselves to the automatic locks on the ground, no one could enter or exit. If a Lock Down was announced, one must make it to the closest building and wait out the storm. Almost every time a storm came, some person or persons would risk taking the extra time to get to their home. Those that failed to make it would have their flesh torn off by the one hundred to two hundred mile per hour winds and the harsh texture of the purple sand.

Yuri Gorski, Les Gillis, Michel Evart, Jen Staszko and Elektra Papanikolaou arrived at the Academy Dormitory rooms just before five in the morning. Seward instructed the five cadets to go to their rooms, shower and then take a long nap. Their absence from classes would be excused. The cadets had been through much emotional stress and it showed in their eyes, their gait, their lack of energy and a seeming loss of appetite shared by all five. Seward let the men go to their rooms and he personally escorted the two women to their rooms. He hoped that the idea of a conspiracy or a cover up was just paranoia. He would hate to lose any more cadets.

Les Gillis placed his palm on the wall panel in front of his dormitory quarters door frame and watched as his door slid open to his room. He was thankful that no one was up and walking about, roaming the halls, as he had little desire for interaction. He walked in through his door and was immediately greeted by Cosmos, Love-Easter's beloved black and white cat. Cosmos meowed and rubbed against Gillis' legs. Gillis pet the friendly cat and walked over to his bed and sat down. He noticed Cosmos was looking at the door, meowing and looking back to Gillis. The cat was obviously waiting for Love-Easter to come home. That sight finally broke Gillis down. He slid to the floor on his knees with tears of grief streaming down his face. Cosmos, as if sensing Gillis needed comforting, walked over to him and began rubbing his little head on Gillis arm and licking his hand.

"I am so sorry little buddy," Gillis struggled to get the words out as he pet the cat. "It is just us now. You and me against the Galaxy." Gillis was petting the cat, and realized that the interaction with Cosmos was something that was soothing to him. The cat would meow, walking around Gillis, rubbing his body and face against him. Gillis pet the cat for a long time. Gillis did not care about his classes for the day as he preferred to stay in the room with Cosmos.

Even though Gillis had been gone for over five days, cats were self-sufficient and needed little supervision. Love-Easter and Gillis had bought for Cosmos several balls with bells, catnip toys, and the best state of the art machines. Cosmos had computer controlled food dispensers that would, at a time pre-set by the owner, drop a measured amount of food down a plastic tubing into Cosmos' food bowl. They had purchased the same type of machine for Cosmos' water bowl, which would filter the water every hour for the cat. The cat litter box was even more advanced in the technology. When Cosmos would go to his three foot long by two foot wide litter box, the feces and urine would be vaporized by the granular litter. It had taken many years of scientific research to develop the advancements to perfect the litter to attack the cat waste and not harm the cat. It was completely safe to Cosmos, but was very costly to poor Academy students like Gillis and Love-Easter. Gillis recalled that Love-Easter would always say that any expense was worth buying happiness for Cosmos.

After spending about half an hour petting the friendly cat, Gillis fell asleep on the floor. Cosmos cuddled up against his legs and fell asleep with him. Gillis had been so exhausted that a bomb could have gone off next to him and he would not have heard it.

Yuri Gorski also did not wish to interact with any of his classmates. He made it to his dormitory room without crossing paths with anyone. After his palm and fingerprints were scanned by the security system, his door opened and he walked into his room. His roommate, Drew Harrison was naked on one of the two beds with a naked woman lying next to him. Their clothes were piled together on the floor. Gorski did not recognize the girl and speculated that Harrison must have met her at a party. He deduced that she was a cadet, based on her medical school uniform that was strewn across the floor.

Gorski undressed and slid under the covers of his own bed. He was happy Harrison had met someone new, even if it were just for the night. Gorski's friend had been in a long term relationship which ended and Harrison had been having difficulty dealing with his emotions regarding the break up. The girl, Julia Steiner, had been a member of the Gorski Gang and had been Harrison's sole girlfriend for over two years. Steiner was from Lauterbrunnen, Switzerland, of old Earth and was attractive, very smart and was attending the Academy in the science department. Gorski had no doubt Steiner would be a brilliant scientist one day, in whatever field she decided to specialize in. He missed Steiner as part of the group as she was always the one with the more humane outlook on life. She had compassion for others and an uncanny ability to verbally spar with the best. Steiner had always been loyal to her friends and never backed away from any potential confrontation.

When Steiner and Harrison parted ways, she told Gorski that her decision to end the relationship had to do with Harrison over doing it with the alcohol. Gorski tried to defend Harrison, as he was Gorski's best friend. But in his heart, he knew Steiner had been correct regarding Harrison's alcohol intake. Gorski and all of his friends would drink, especially on weekends, but Harrison had been taking the alcohol consumption to the extremes.

Gorski regarded Harrison, sleeping soundly in his bed. He could smell the whiskey in the room. Harrison had been drinking alcohol much more than normal and last night seemed to have been more of the same. Steiner had begged Harrison to go cold turkey or get help. He refused her requests. Gorski also had tried to convince Harrison to seek out counseling or some outpatient treatment for his own well-being. Harrison also refused him, telling Gorski that there was no problem.

Now Steiner was heavily involved with one of the Collins boys. She had moved on with her life with someone else and no longer associated with the Gorski Gang. Harrison knew she was in a new relationship and it hurt the man deeply. Harrison loved Steiner and he did not know how to cope with losing her. Gorski closed his weary eyes. He decided it was time to get some sleep and worry about his friend Drew Harrison later.

Michel Evart made it to his dormitory room without meeting any other person. Evart was grateful for that as he was far too exhausted to interact with others. He had decided before he went to sleep he would try to connect a live broadcast through the campus computer system to let his sister, Flora, know he was home safe. Evart entered his room and heard the shower being used. His roommate, Jack Harcourt, was generally an early riser. No one else was in the room.

Evart sat on his bed and began his attempt to contact Flora. He asked his computer to make a person to person connection with her. Within two minutes, Flora's face appeared on the three dimensional monitor. She was rubbing her eyes, having been awakened by her computer.

"Hello?" Flora Evart was drowsy, her eyes red from all of the crying.

"Hey baby sister," Evart said to her. "Good morning."

Flora's eyes widened at the sound of his voice. "Michel! Is that really you?"

"Yes, it is me. I am sorry for waking you so early. But I wanted to let you know that I was back in the dorm room and safe."

"But the news said you were dead!" Flora could not control her joy at hearing the voice of her older brother. He was her closest sibling, the one that always protected her. She had spent the entire night crying at the news he was dead. Now, hearing his voice and seeing his face, she was wide awake, feeling as if she were ready to take on the world.

"No, I am alive. The others are home safe as well," Michel told her. He was feeling the lack of sleep taking him over. "I will meet you for dinner tonight? I have a great adventure to share with you."

"Ah, Michel, I was so heartbroken. I thought I had lost my big brother. Yes, yes, dinner tonight! I want to hear everything." She was always excited to hear of her older brother's tales. She had been made one of the Gorski Gangs honorable members. But, since she was only seventeen, she was not allowed to enter the bars or some of the other places Michel and their friends would frequent. So, Flora lived vicariously through the stories Michel would relate to her about the adventures of the group.

"Till tonight," Michel said as he struggled to stay awake. "Say six o'clock at Casa Franco's?"

"Yes, I will be there! I love you!"

"I love you too," Michel said and terminated the communication broadcast.

Evart started to lie down when Jack Harcourt entered the room. He had a white towel wrapped around his body which was the same color as his milky white skin, his hair still wet and dripping.

"What the hell?" Harcourt said when he saw Evart. "Michel!"

"In the flesh my friend!" Evart stood as Harcourt rushed to embrace his roommate.

"But how?" Harcourt was stunned. "They made Blossom Li and I take over yours and Yuri's flight units. Everyone heard on the news that..."

Evart cut him off with a wave of his hand, "The news was wrong my friend. Somehow our names were listed on that Transport. We found out we were 'dead' when we landed on New Edinburgh by private flight. I am so sorry we did not call everyone, but it was about two in the morning when we arrived. We felt it best to wait for the morning."

"You need to tell Flora, she was a mess last night," Harcourt said as he began dressing into his cadet flight suit. "And the others, April, Marco, Mary, the whole group."

"We will tell everyone, of course," Evart assured his friend. "But, the five of us really needed some sleep. Can you get the word out for me? Let the others know that we are all still alive?"

"Do not worry my friend. I will let the cadet pilots know today at formation." Harcourt was pulling on his boots as he spoke. "It is wonderful to see you again."

"It is good to be seen," Evart responded, knowing that had Garrison not intervened he may well have been dead. "Sit down; I have things I must tell you."

Despite the warnings of Colonel Gorski, Evart had already determined that Jack Harcourt could be trusted completely. Evart told his roommate everything. Harcourt listened intently to his friend as he related the events of the past few days.

Elektra Papanikolaou and Jen Staszko entered their dormitory building together. They walked across the foyer of grey tiled walls and white floors, passing the front desk, hoping to avoid any and all contact with other students. After making it to their dorm room, they sat down on their beds, kicking off their shoes. They were both exhausted. Their room was one of the cleanest in the entire dormitory system. Yuri sometimes jokingly accused Staszko of being a "germiphobe." Both of the women were always cleaning and washing. Their beds were always made up, their clothes hung neatly in their individual walk-in closets. But on that morning, they were both so drained of energy that they threw their clothing onto the floor and went to sleep.

The news spread rapidly around the Academy that the five Gorski Gang members returned to New Edinburgh very much alive. Some cadets called them the Fab Five or Five Alive or other nicknames. There was a general happiness spreading around the university with the exception of the Bragg Gang members. William Bragg and his brother Bret were joyful the night before that Gorski, Evart and Gillis were dead. William Bragg had speculated that Gorski's demise would leave a void in leadership and enable the Bragg's to become the dominant group on campus. Hearing that the hated cadets were still alive sent him into a rage. He took his anger out on his wife, Yesenia Guevara, by beating her before he left for class.

While others rejoiced in the return of the five presumed dead cadets, one other cadet did not. He heard the news and scowled. The handsome cadet with long blonde hair down to the small of his back walked off of the campus area toward the area in Clovis City that new buildings were being built. He stood over six feet five inches tall and had deep blue eyes. He was very muscular from his time as a weightlifter and steroid abuser. He watched the area around him like a hawk.

The construction was fast paced. Clovis City had plenty of empty acres to build on. The cadet walked past a set of four buildings being constructed side by side by side by side. They were scheduled to stand ninety-five floors high. The foundation and the metal frames were already in place. The construction workers and architects were already up, working against deadlines to erect the four skyscrapers. Large pallets of tiles, lumber and cement mix were all around. Ships of varying sizes were flying in with pre-constructed walls connected by towing cables to better guide the walls to the metal frames where workers would drill the walls to the metal. Many of the construction workers were using jet packs on their backs to fly in the air and help guide the giant walls to the structure. Once the wall was against the metal frames, they would drill them firmly into place with solar powered machines. Standing on the roof tops of the massive buildings were soldiers, wielding laser rifles, watching the skies for the deadly Cawlers that would sometimes hunt humans.

Once the cadet felt that he was far enough away from campus, he pulled out of his uniform breast pocket a hand sized, blue metal holo-com device. He made sure he found a quiet area where the sound of the construction would not impede his conversation. He looked over his back, and saw he had not been followed.

"Computer, connect me to Space Station Cy-7, Hotel Baroness, chief of security," the young man spoke into the device. "High priority."

Ella Ragnarsson was already at her desk in her security office. She had a slight hangover from the champagne the night before. She had a twenty ounce cup of vanilla latte on her desk top as she sat down. Her staff knew that first thing in the morning, she had to have her favorite coffee drink, or someone would suffer the consequences.

Ella took a sip and licked her lips. The warm coffee drink was like ambrosia to her. The computer alerted Ella that she had a high priority call from her brother on New Edinburgh. Ella set the coffee cup down. "Three dimensional face to face, please."

A holographic image of Ella Ragnarsson appeared before the cadet. "Good morning Ella, it's me, Ivar."

"Good morning Ivar," Ella greeted her little brother, looking at his image. "Why are you not in your classes? Father told you that he expects perfect grades."

"Forget class, sis!" Ivar said quickly. "I have news from the campus."

"Be rude then!" Ella snapped back at him. Ivar was always an impatient little cretin. Ella loved all of her siblings, but she always found it difficult to interact with Ivar. "What is more important than your school work? Why would you skip out on your weapons training?"

Ivar sighed. His family always lectured him. He was the youngest of the siblings and he never got any respect from any of the others. They always treated him like he was a little child. Ivar never grew used to his family pushing him to do this or that. The way Ella was speaking to him was typical. "Look, sis. I got news. Just now heard it from some of the other students. Those five cadets that died in the Transport accident. Remember them?"

Ella picked up her cup and took a drink of her coffee. She had told Ivar the night before that it had been a family sponsored job to eliminate the five cadets. "Yes, Ivar, I remember. I suppose you are calling to tell me all of the other cadets are crying and whining and holding each other as if the deaths can be cured with a stupid hug and words from an incompetent, no talent, hack clergyman. What is it Ivar? Why are you not in class?"

"Sis, the five cadets? They were not on that Transport. They are back on campus. You guys fucked up. They are alive."

Ella gasped and dropped her coffee cup to the floor. Her coffee spilled as she sucked in a deep breath. "What did you say?"

"The five cadets are still alive. You all did not get them."

Ella breathed in heavily. The Rosenburgs and her father did not take failure lightly. When the word of this got out, there would be plenty of angry people and there would be a demand to get the job done properly this time around. Emma Ragnarsson might even suffer some form of punishment for her failure.

"And this is confirmed?" Ella wanted to be certain before she began making the necessary contact calls.

"I heard it from one of the roommate's mouth," Ivar said. "They are here, on campus and very much alive."

Ella was silent for a few seconds. After a few seconds of thought about what to do about the information, she cursed and stood up. "Ivar, go back to class. Be a good student. Do not, and I mean this, do not get involved in this. Understand?"

"But I am ready!" Ivar assured Ella. "I can help!"

"Ivar, you are to do nothing!" Ella barked at him. "You need to learn to stop questioning what I tell you to do. Why can't you follow orders? Do not go near those five cadets. Father would be very angry with you if you do anything without authorization. Go back to class and do nothing. Remember, you are the one that father wants to have a long military career. Our family needs to have a ranking officer in the Space Command. That means that you go to class, study and stay out of family business. You will be a great help to us when you start advancing in rank. When that day comes, then you will be brought in to help. You hear me, Ivar?"

"Yes, Ella. I will do nothing. I will go back to class now." Ivar turned off his hand held Holo-com and began walking back to the campus. He would do as he was told and be a good student, go to class, study but he would also participate in the Gorski Gang dinner celebrations, against Ella's wishes. Ivar intended to get in close to the enemy despite the promise he made to his older sister.

As soon as she finished her conversation with Ivar, Ella Ragnarsson rushed to the office of Penelope Smith. If what Ivar told her was true, then the proverbial crap would hit the fan.

Ella told the computer to open the doors to Penelope's office. She spied the room and Penelope was not there. It was out of character for Penelope to be late for work as she was always early and a workaholic. Ella desperately needed to speak to someone. She ran back to her own office and sealed the doors shut behind her. She could not fathom how it was that Emma had failed. The plan had been perfect. Ella did not want the Rosenburg's to punish her sister for allowing the cadets to escape. She had to find a way to make sure that the targets were killed without Alfred Rosenburg learning of the failure at the space station. She considered her options carefully as to who she could trust and who she could not.

Ella decided to contact the one man in the entire Empire that had never failed to kill a target, Dell Ragnarsson, her father. Dell Ragnarsson was the most feared assassin alive. He had been involved in hundreds of killings and had never been caught, never even suspected. Law enforcement had no pictures or fingerprints on file for Dell Ragnarsson. His DNA had never been secured at any of his missions by the incompetent police forces. Ella would get her father to assist and then the five cadets would all die, one by one.

CHAPTER FIVE

Admiral Seward had been summoned to meet with the Dean of the Academy and dutifully reported. The administrative building for the Academy was one of the many tall towers in Clovis City that decorated the skyline. After being admitted to the top floor where the Dean and his staff worked, Seward was directed to the main conference room. He took a seat at the long table and waited for Dean Golden Harvard to join him. The room was about forty feet long and thirty feet thick. There were two round tables at the east and west side of the room, a sink with fresh coffee on and pastries. Harvard arrived at a minute before the scheduled start of the meeting. The two exchanged pleasantries. A secretary entered the room and served coffee to the two men. They waited in silence until Professors Abcde Rand, Drea Kirby and Jaksen Warren walked into the room. The five were the top leaders of Clovis Academy. Seward, the chief pilot instructor, Rand was the Dean of the Engineering section, Kirby was Dean of the Science Department and taught advanced physics, and Warren was the Dean of the Law School and taught ethics and Empire Treaty Law.

Seward liked dealing with Professor Warren as he was a straight shooter and had a great sense of humor. Warren's wife was the Dean of the Pre-Medical section and well-liked by the students. While the majority of men had multiple wives, Warren loved his one and only. He would never dream of bringing another woman into his life. They had moved to Clovis City to help start up the new Academy and remained ever since. Jaksen Warren was a close friend and confidant to Sean Collins; the latter graciously guest lecturing at the Law School whenever the invitation was extended.

Professor Kirby was quiet and unassuming. Her hair was never combed and looked as if it had never been washed. She was skinny as a rail and had pale skin. She did not dress in the traditional business attire or military uniforms as the majority of the professors. Kirby only wore orange or red one piece jump suits, claiming that it was for pragmatic reasons. Her method of teaching the science students was to get into the dirt, oil and chemical experiments with the cadets to demonstrate how to be better scientists.

The only one that Seward disliked was Rand. She had been accused by several female students of demanding sex in return for a passing grade. Rand vehemently denied each and every accusation and countered that the cadets were attempting to blackmail her to give a passing grade. Seward had never been on the review teams to determine if the individual cadet claims were true or not. But the number of complaints against Rand gave Seward an inkling that the cadets might be the victims of a professor abusing her power over them.

Harvard had previously asked the four to produce a list of candidates to be selected for the Tournament on Semiramis Moon. Ten cadets would be selected to represent Clovis Academy at the event. Harvard demanded that each of the four Dean's produced a list of thirty cadets and then they could collaborate together and pare down the list. The event was to occur in March, which was only a few months away. The prevailing wisdom was to put together a team early, get them training together so that they would know each other's strengths and weaknesses and so that they would learn to work in harmony with one another.

The previous year, Clovis Academy finished in last place out of the four Academy competitors. Tyr Academy had won the previous year, capturing the cadets from all the other three schools. Clovis Academy was caught first and forced to surrender. Harvard did not want that to happen again as he considered a last place finish an embarrassment.

All of the professors were poured a cup of coffee by a secretary whether they wanted it or not. There was a plate with fresh fruit on the center of the table.

"Gentle ladies and men," Harvard said, tapping his fingers on his list. "I gave each of you an assignment to list thirty qualified cadets for the Tournament. We need to mutually decide today who our ten member team will be."

Rand set her laptop computer on the table and accessed her files pertaining to the list she had prepared for the Tournament Team. All of the others assembled pulled out legal pads, each with names scribbled on the first page.

Professor Warren was the first to speak, "Golden, my wife and I spoke and felt it best to leave the five pilot slots on the team to be selected by Admiral Seward. It would not be right for us to second guess his assessment of the talent level of the pilots since we have little interaction with them. I would only say that Professor Rand highly recommends Mary Lincoln and Porfirio Cardenas as two of the pilots since they both are capable as mechanical engineers from the required Engine Technician classes. We checked them out and learned that they both have high grade points and are both graduating seniors."

Harvard looked to Seward, "Any objection to Lincoln and Cardenas on the team?"

Seward smiled, "No objection at all. My original list was for Lincoln, Cardenas, Evart, Gorski, Al-Nasser, Jack Harcourt, Blossom Li, Alan Rhinehard and Marco Andolini. After what happened to cadet al-Nasser, I have been struggling for another name worthy of the challenge. I came up with a younger cadet, Jurgen Doernitz. He and Andolini both displayed unusual bravery in the Forbidden Region flight."

Rand shook her head up and down, "Doernitz is also a star engineering student. He would be acceptable to me."

"So, of that list, which five would you recommend as the pilots for the competition?" Harvard demanded of Seward.

"Lincoln and Cardenas, for the reasons Warren stated." Seward said. "Andolini for certain and Rhinehard for his abilities. I most certainly think Evart and Gorski should also go."

"That would be six pilots!" Rand blurted out. "We only need five."

Seward shook his head, "With all due respect, this idea of doing what we always do is why we never win the competition. Each of you said you wanted Lincoln and Cardenas because of their other talents. I suggest to each of you that the six I selected are more than just pilots. All six are capable hand to hand fighters. They have studied either boxing, martial arts or wrestling techniques. If you really want to win this Tournament, we need multi-talented fighters, real scrapers that are not afraid of getting their hands dirty. I already selected your ten man/woman team, Dean Harvard. And, I really believe my list is a winner."

Professor Kirby, who had been silent all this time, finally spoke. "As a scientist, I would never be presumptuous enough to step into your field of expertise, Admiral Seward, which is unmitigated warfare. You fought many famous battles before you retired. You led men and women into battle. You had victories. So, I know I would be most interested in discussing your list first, with an eye on the ten best cadets that will have the guts to capture the enemy."

Seward was happy Kirby was there. The physicist was a brilliant teacher. None of the others would dare debate her.

Harvard nodded, "Let's hear it, Seward. Give us your list."

"Thank you. I selected doctoral candidate Eamon O'Grady as the team leader. O'Grady has a perfect grade point average and will finish his doctorate in May.   He is smart, athletic, and an expert in weapons technology. He is a marksman with both the laser rifle and hand laser. I checked into his training scores and they are excellent. His leadership tests showed no signs of weakness.

"Second in command would be Yuri Gorski. He is a graduating senior with a dual major in military intelligence and flight command. His grades are solid. But, we all know he is a natural born leader. Other cadets gravitate to Gorski, they respect and follow him. He is also a great fighter. You all know that he has been in some bar fights which resulted in a demotion in rank and some demerits. I ask each of you to not look upon his fights as a negative, but a positive. Remember those rowdy illegal weapons dealers from last year that started a brawl at the Hades Hall Bar last year? Gorski and his friends were outnumbered five to one and beat them down. Gorski and his friends did not start the fight, but they sure knew how to finish it. Plus, over the summer, Gorski followed his parents' footsteps and completed the Spetsnaz Special Forces training.

"Third in command would be Porfirio Cardenas and I would select him as the pilot chief. He also has strong leadership ability and is very skilled at directing other pilots during stressful situations.

"My list finished out with the following seven cadets: Mary Lincoln, Marco Andolini, Klaus Rhinehard, Lester Gillis, Drew Harrison, Michel Evart and Julia Steiner."

"Why Gillis, Harrison and Steiner?" Rand was rubbing her hands together.

"Because Gillis is a military history brain. He knows tactics, weaponry and he also is a great hand to hand fighter. He also has other talents. He walks in many worlds at the Academy and is friends with O'Grady and Gorski. We all know O'Grady and Gorski have their own little groups on the campus. Gillis is the only one accepted by both. Because of that fact, our two commanders will listen to Gillis and his council, if it ever becomes needed. He also has a great working knowledge of computer programing. He speaks several languages. Gillis is knowledgeable in first aid, medical needs and has some experience in the medical field.

"Harrison is also a military weapons expert and he is a first rate investigator. He has a great understanding of computer technology. He is a fighter and is possibly the strongest cadet on campus. He has some of the highest marksmanship scores on campus. Each of you should watch him in the free weight section of the campus gymnasium. I have and that kid can out bench press the whole lot of us. He also has studied some of the life sciences classes and can do more than render the average first aid.

"Steiner is one of the best science students on campus. She is a computer expert, studied medical classes and I understand can even perform some minor surgeries. She will be valuable in that she knows the nutritional needs of the team, the medical needs and she is also a fighter. She was involved in that infamous brawl last year between Gorski's Gang and those rogue pilots. I understand Steiner knocked out three men twice her size. Any of you want to fight her and see how tough she is?"

"We will pass and take your word for it," Rand said. "Now, you are assuming that your list of ten will accept the challenge. What if one or more say no?"

Seward nodded, as he had expected the question. "I propose we have about five alternates, in case one or more either say no or bow out or get injured. I put down Dominic Andolini who is an outstanding marksman, Jurgen Doernitz who is a pilot and an engineer, Sophia DuBravac who is one of our better engineering and security cadets, Blossom Li who is a pilot and medical doctor candidate, Jack Harcourt who is a double major in pilot section and weaponry and my last alternate was Mia Nguyen who is a computer expert and performed well in the last holographic war games competition. Nguyen also is a formidable hand to hand fighter."

Rand grunted, "You got it all figured out. We didn't even have to be here. What about Reynita Calderon? She is quite a markswoman herself."

Harvard shook his head. Rand always had to start trouble between her and Seward. Plus, all of the Professors were aware that Rand had slept with Reynita Calderon over a year ago. It had caused a bit of a scandal when it was revealed Rand threatened Calderon with a failing grade if she did not perform sexual favors. Calderon complied with the demands of her Professor to avoid being flunked from her class. Unfortunately for Professor Rand, Calderon's brothers and sisters caught onto the scheme and made official complaints which resulted in Professor Rand being suspended without pay for a month. Harvard had wanted to fire Rand from his staff but the union protected her. Harvard was forced to keep Rand on due to the union pressure. The Calderon family was understandably angered by the outcome.

Harvard determined that including Rand in the selection process might have been a mistake on his part. "Look, everyone leave your lists with me. I will make the final selection by tomorrow morning. We will announce to the cadets the selections on Friday. I want this done so this year we can compete for once. Tyr Academy has three returning cadets from last year's championship team. They will be ready. We need to be better than them. I am growing weary of our Academy finishing in last place each year."

With that, the meeting was over. Understanding that Harvard detested long winded meetings or discussions, the professors filed out of the room, leaving Seward and Harvard alone.

"Sir, the word is out regarding the five returning cadets," Seward said softly so his voice would not carry.

"I know, Admiral," Harvard stood up collecting the lists left behind by the other Professors. "The five guards are in place. I hope nothing happens. I do not want any more deaths. Losing cadets al-Nasser and Love-Easter is enough for the year. I have already received demands for information from the Education Secretary on Sikorsky's Planet. There is going to be some Court of Inquiries convened over both student deaths. I guess bad news travels quickly between planets. If you need me, I will be in my office responding to those inquiries."

Seward hoped the same in that there would be no further loss of life. But neither man could predict the shadow of evil being cast over the Clovis Academy and the imminent violence that was yet to come. Neither man would have ever predicted that a family of well-trained assassins were planning on turning the campus into a war zone.

Dirk Fenster had rolled out of his bed and saw that Arch Frazier had made it back to the room. Ann Harcourt was still asleep next to Fenster. Frazier was also sleeping like a baby. Fenster walked to the shower and took his time getting ready to face the day. After Fenster had dressed, he saw that Frazier was still asleep. Fenster decided to leave and let his friend sleep the day away. Fenster decided to not wake up Ann Harcourt either. It was not the first time she had spent the night with Fenster and she knew the way out.

Fenster darted out of his dormitory room into the hallway and walked rapidly to the stairs. He descended the staircase to the lower level and exited the men's dormitory to feel the wind in his face. The granular purple sand of New Edinburgh was whipping around the campus. Fenster covered his face as he ran toward the cafeteria for his late breakfast and coffee. Fenster was hoping that the winds were not a sign of a coming sandstorm. The winds could twist as high as three hundred kilometers per hour. The storms were infamous on New Edinburgh and had been the cause of much destruction and loss of life.

Fenster strode into the campus cafeteria and dusted off the purple sand from his clothing. There were several cadets in the "chow line" getting bacon, eggs, pancakes, French toast, fruits, cereals, muffins, juices and coffee. Fenster saw Klaus Rhinehard and April Mejia sitting together, with trays of food around them. Mejia noticed Fenster and waved him over. Fenster moved through the crowd of cadets to join his two friends and sat down at their long table.

"The winds are getting really bad out there," Fenster told them. "Frazier was in his bed, out cold. He looked like he pulled an all-nighter studying."

"Yes, it might be a sand storm coming. The margarita's you made last night must have been potent," Mejia told him. "We are the first three here. Everyone else is still passed out."

Fenster laughed, "Well, I never said I was a professional bartender. Is the food good this morning?"

"The French toast is really good. I had six pieces." Klaus told him.

"Good, I love French toast." Fenster stood up and excused himself. He made his way to the line of cadets filling their trays with their first of three square meals for the day. Being a cadet had benefits; the food at the Clovis Academy cafeteria was excellent.

Fenster filled his tray and picked up a large coffee and apple juice. He rejoined Mejia and Klaus, who were holding hands. Fenster deduced the couple had taken their relationship to the next level. Good for them, Fenster thought. His mind drifted back to his friend, Frazier. He also had found a good woman in Papanikolaou. Fenster was concerned about his best friend in that he had lost the girl before the relationship could blossom.

Fenster sat with his two friends, tearing into the French toast with his knife and fork, "You were right, the toast is great. Any news?"

"No news, my friend," Klaus replied. "Oh, wow."

"What?" Mejia asked.

"Look," Klaus motioned with his head to the door. Mejia and Fenster looked to see Marco Andolini and Mary Lincoln walking toward the chow line, holding hands, laughing and whispering in each other's ears.

"Holy Texas. Marco and Mary. Together?" Fenster asked the others. "I never saw that one coming."

Mejia poked Fenster on the arm, "You better get with it Dirk. All the available women are being taken off the market."

"It's a big universe and there are at least eight girls for every guy," Fenster shrugged. The truth was that Fenster was not ready for any serious relations. His parents had high expectations for him and he wanted to make sure that if he ever did bring a woman home to meet them, that she was the one. Plus, he trusted very few people. He had a huge trust fund from his family money. He was always suspicious of the women that seemed to know who he was and where he had come from. Mejia was correct about one thing, it seemed like all of the women that Fenster would consider taking home to mom were already involved with someone else.

Les Gillis took a shower after he woke up from his short sleep. The howling winds of the approaching New Edinburgh sand storm had caused him to wake up. He dried off and pulled on a blue sweater, with breast pockets, khaki cargo pants and black boots. Cosmos was following Gillis as he walked back and forth. Gillis picked up the small back pack given to him by Giles Lancer and opened it to inspect the contents. Inside were several stun darts, arm and leg binders, some knives and a few flame darts. All five of the cadets took some of the items on the Blues City space craft just in case trouble came their way. Arch Frazier also took some so he could help out if need be. Gillis put two stun darts in his breast pocket of his sweater. He pocketed a set of arm and leg binders, just in case.

Gillis then decided to continue what he had started back on the space station. "Computer, display three dimensional computer keyboard. Connect to campus e-mail."

A green type pad appeared before Gillis. He typed in Penelope Smith's e-mail address and sent her a letter. He let her know he enjoyed the time they spent together and that he hoped to meet her again soon. He wished her well and expressed his desire to hear from her. He pressed "Send" and asked the computer to display the climatology report. Gillis read the bad news. There was a possible sand storm moving in the direction of Clovis City. That would mean the entire city and Academy would be on weather alert and a possible Lock Down would be ordered by the climatologists. Everyone would be confined to housing until the storm passed. Gillis terminated the computer connection.

"Cosmos, I must go see my other friends. I will be back quickly."

Gillis pet the cat on his stomach as Cosmos was stretched out on his back. Gillis left his dorm room with a sense of urgency. He had to warn the others to be hyper-vigilant. Gillis had read about a village on planet Cootron in which an assassination team successfully used the cover of bad weather to conceal their actions. There was also the past event on Clovis City known as Dark October where a team of assassins used a lightning storm as cover to kill some high ranking military officers. Since a sand storm could take a day or two to pass through the city that would be more than enough time for a skilled killer to get the job done.

Dell Ragnarsson, Jr., was thirty-one years old. His family and friends called him Junior to avoid confusion between him and his father. He had learned from his father that there were over a million ways to kill a man or woman. Junior had also learned that if one became talented enough at the art of assassination, then the money would come easy. There was always someone with disposable cash that desired to have another person permanently removed from the chess board of life. He had been taught by his own father who was considered in many circles as the best assassin alive. Father and son had completed dozens of missions together. His father never failed and Junior had a similar record of success. Although Junior did not have the extensive resume of his father, his was still formidable for presentation to potential employers. His organization and execution of the Dark October killings made him a highly sought after hit man. He was receiving work and money so quickly that he had to expand his network.

The primary paying clients for his father and family were the Rosenburg's and the Sikorsky's. The Royal Family had many needs for the services of swift killings so that they could maintain their two hundred year rule over humanity. Whenever that family had a need, the Ragnarsson's were to make them a priority. Junior trained daily and was lifting weights in his private five floor mansion on Rosenburg's Ranch when he received the communication from his computer that an incoming broadcast was waiting for him. He finished his set of twenty curls and set down the two barbells of one hundred pounds each. He picked up a towel and wiped the sweat out of his eyes. One of his wives was in the large gymnasium with him. She was his fifth wife, provided to him by the Rosenburg family as a reward for a job well done. Junior had earned his large mansion from the wealthy family for work he had done for the Rosenburg's over the years. Many times the Rosenburg's would have a beautiful young woman as a bonus for a him. They gave him two lovely nineteen year old twins for his work on the Dark October mission. Junior was happy to take the women for his own pleasure, marry them and produce offspring.

Junior asked his computer system to display the priority message. A three dimensional image of Dell Ragnarsson Senior, Junior's father, appeared before him. The image began speaking, "Son, I have a priority mission for you. I need for you to go to Clovis City and take out five targets on the Clovis Academy campus. I have encrypted a file attached to this broadcast with the names and pictures of the five targets. This must be done tonight. There is a report of a sand storm that might hit Clovis City. If the storm system does turn in the direction of the City, that would be perfect cover for the assignment. Ivar is on the campus and can show you around. Take Emma with you, she needs to redeem herself. We need this done, it is a matter of professionalism that we complete our contracts. Emma needs to learn that lesson. I would do it myself, but I am a few days flight away. I know you can handle this."

The image disappeared. Junior instructed the computer to notify Emma that he would pick her up at her mansion in five minutes. Junior quickly decided that he would take a squad of five men that had worked with him many times before. He purchased his five floor mansion so that he could house his wives, children, weaponry, training rooms and assemble men and women that would be loyal to him. There were five such loyal killers on the premises. It was time for them to earn their keep as they had done so on many missions before.

He looked over at his fifth wife, Dulce, who was running on a computerized treadmill. She was in her early twenties, attractive, and had been learning how to be a killer under his teaching. Dulce had grown up as a second generation slave on the Rosenburg Ranch. Junior was able to convince the Rosenburg family to give Dulce to him as part payment on a past job. Dulce was willing to do anything to avoid a beating and learned everything that he requested.

"Dulce," Junior said to her. "Shower and suit up. We have a priority mission. It is time you went out in the field with me."

Dulce obediently stopped her running, grabbed her towel and began walking toward the showers. She had trained for the last year in the art of hand to hand combat and close quarters brawls with knives. She was ready to kill if needed, not because she wished to kill, but to avoid another beating from her heartless husband.

Junior and his team of five mercenaries had recently returned from the planet Cootron on an assignment to kill four politicians that were advocating cessation from the Earth Empire. One of the traitors was the Secretary General of the General Assembly of Cootron's United Nations. She had long believed that the Sikorsky rule for almost two hundred Earth years should end. Now she was dead due to a boiler room explosion that was caused by Junior and his hit men. The other three rebellious politicians died in freak accidents, designed by Junior and his team. It took them three weeks on Cootron to plan, coordinate and execute the mission.

They did not fail. All four of the conspirators were no longer a threat to the rule of the Glorious Leader of the Earth Empire, Vladimir Sikorsky.

He instructed his mansion computer system to notify his team. It was time to serve the Royal Family and kill again. There would be no room for failure.

The Raumschiff was ready when Junior boarded. Dulce was already on board. She had her camouflage outfit on, with a utility belt wrapped around her that was filled with several knives and a laser pistol. The five men that Junior had relied on in past missions were also on board checking their weapons and making small talk.

One of his favorite team members was a man called Nikko Xian. Nikko was in his forties and had served with Junior's father and now served the son. Nikko had several scars on his body from many past battles. He had small death skulls tattooed on his arms; each skull represented a confirmed kill. He was an accurate shooter and good hand to hand combat expert. He followed orders and never complained. Nikko had last served with Junior on the mission to Cootron. Junior liked Nikko on a personal level as they enjoyed playing chess against each other. Nikko also had several children on different planets from different women. Nikko never wanted to settle down with any of the mothers. He enjoyed taking lives much more than raising a family.

The second member of the team was a man named Vinnie Montrose. Montrose was seven feet tall and built with solid muscle. Junior had watched Montrose break a man's back by slamming the victim onto a concrete wall. He was silent, fast on his feet and a loyal hand to have on a mission such as this one. Montrose walked with confidence, his short hair was combed and not a strand out of place. The only flaw was his crooked nose which had been broken several times in the past. Montrose rarely spoke of his personal life. In fact, he rarely spoke at all. There had been a rumor that Montrose had been sexually involved with one of the Rosenburg women named Nydia. Whether the rumor was true or not was none of Junior's concern. As long as Montrose did his part on each mission then his personal life was his own business.

The team explosives expert was Raul de Tigre Quintana. He was just as deadly as the others. His primary talent was as a master of rigging explosives. Anytime they needed for a murder to look like an accidental event, Quintana was the man Junior turned to. Quintana was older than the others, but never revealed his exact age. Junior speculated that Quintana was in his late forties. The explosives expert spoke seven languages and had been a talented opera singer before choosing the more profitable life of a mercenary. Quintana had revealed once that he was a widower and had left his children at an orphanage to free himself for a life of travel and adventure.   The fourth team member was originally from the planet New Vladivostok. Chang had been a wanted man in three planetary systems for random acts of violence. Junior's father took Chang in, arranged a name change and plastic surgery on his face so that he could travel without fear of recognition. Chang had killed men and women by many different methods. He alternated knives, lasers, ice pick, fire or simply throwing a person out of an air lock in deep space. Chang did not care how the job was done, as long as it was successful. He never spoke of family or friends except to comment that family was a luxury that assassins could not afford to have. He never revealed his name to the others and when questioned as to whether or not Chang was his first or last name, he would always respond with a "Yes" and refuse to answer any further inquiries on the subject.

And then there was the Englishman, Prescott. He was as ruthless as the others, but was generally polite about it. Prescott was a former military intelligence soldier with Ranger training in the York Militia. He was handsome, slim with good muscle tone. He would kill a person while smiling at them. Prescott enjoyed using a garrote on victims, sneaking up behind them and strangling the target to death. The only criticism Junior had of Prescott was that he had an explosive temper that would become evident if things started to grow too stressful. Prescott had been sleeping with Emma Ragnarsson off and on for the last two years. Although Junior was aware of and accepted their relationship, he knew his father would not. Father wanted his daughters to marry men of influence and power. If father ever learned that his daughter Emma was sleeping with a hired killer then there would be hell to pay.

Prescott and Emma were cuddled up close on the leather seats of the ship and whispering in each other's ears. Occasionally Emma would laugh out loud in response to something Prescott had told her. Vinnie Montrose pursed his lips as he watched the scene and turned away from the two to face Junior.

"This will be similar to Dark October," Montrose told him.

"Because we are using the weather change to our advantage?" Junior asked him.

"That and that we are going back to Clovis City. If we have time to take dinner at Rubino's on the south side of the city we should. The lasagna there is the best."

"We can worry about food later, Vinnie."

"When I get my hands on some of those young nubile cadet

women I will use them for an appetizer."

"Keep your mind on the mission, Vinnie. If you see a cadet that you like I give you permission to stun her and take her back to the Ranch to use as you wish."

"You are a great employer to work for, Junior."

"Just pick a pretty girl this time."

"The girl I kidnaped from Cootron was cute."

"No, she was not."

Montrose frowned at his friend, "Just because she was cross eyed you think she was ugly?"

"That and her big nose, thick eye brows, pale complexion, no tits, and I am sure I can think of a few other faults that she had."

"You are mean spirited, Junior."

Junior laughed. Montrose was infamous for his lack of mercy to his victims, especially young children. During a mission to Mars, Montrose killed twelve kids that were the children of one of their targets. On Cootron, Montrose wired explosives to a large school transport and blew up fifty elementary school children just to kill two that were offspring of their target. During the Dark October mission, Montrose helped Junior kill all of the children and step-children of Admiral Casados. If anyone on the ship was mean spirited, it was Montrose.

Junior had gone on many missions with his team of killers. They never failed to kill their prey. Junior leaned back in his chair and continued to joke around with Montrose for the remainder of the flight. The five students at Clovis Academy were already dead, he thought to himself. They just didn't know it yet.

CHAPTER SIX

Yuri Gorski showered, shaved and dressed quickly. As he entered the main bedroom, he noticed that Drew Harrison was sitting in a chair, drinking a cup of coffee and downing pain killers for his hangover. The woman that Harrison had over for the night already left after an angry tirade because Harrison could not remember her name to introduce her to his roommate.

"Drew, you really should start cutting back on the booze," Gorski admonished his friend.

"Don't lecture me again, Yuri," Harrison waived his hand at him. Gorski had this discussion a month prior with Harrison.

"I am just saying, that girl was very pretty. She had a nurse's uniform so she clearly had some formal education." Gorski motioned at their closed door for dramatic effect. "She was really steamed that you did not even know her name. You will never keep a woman around if you keep forgetting names."

Harrison turned in his chair and looked at Gorski. His eyes were bloodshot and he seemed to be depressed in the manner he spoke. "Yuri, I don't even remember meeting that girl. I can't remember having sex with her. I do not remember anything about last night except eating dinner at April and Harumi's dorm room, doing tequila shots and drinking Fenster's potent margaritas. I remember Flora being upset when she heard the news that you and her brother were dead. I started drinking whiskey and then sometime after that, I must have blacked out." Harrison was massaging his head in between each of his sentences. This hangover was particularly brutal.

Gorski sat down next to his friend, "Well, let's take things a day at a time. No more drinking until the weekend and when you do drink, you do so in moderation. No more binges, no more shots. Just get an ale and sip it, nurse it, make it last for an hour or two. You do not need to be blacking out any more, especially now. I need you, Drew. I need you to be on your toes and sharp as a knife. So no more going crazy with the liquor. Agreed?"

Harrison massaged his neck and nodded, "Agreed."

"Good, because I need you Drew, like never before. I have a bad feeling that we are going to be targets. The people that killed Dray have connections. When they learn that we escaped the space station, they will come after us. I am going to get Jen to stay here with me so I can better protect her. I need your brains and your muscle. I need your savvy."

Harrison finished off his coffee, "You really think that these people are going to come for you? They already got the cover up they wanted.

The whole investigation was closed, Yuri. They already announced to the world that Drayton's killer confessed. Why would they risk more attention by killing five more cadets?"

Gorski picked up a fresh cup of coffee that Harrison had poured for him and took a sip. "I have had that thought as well, that whoever it is will leave us alone. But if they study our group, they will know we would not let what happened to Dray go. Because of that reason alone, they will have to move on us. Then there is the other reason. Elektra stabbed one of their number. I know I broke the bigger man's arm. Revenge, Drew. Revenge is one hell of a motivator. Plus, there was something in the eyes of one of them, their leader. He had crazy looking eyes, Drew. He was angry, livid, that we stopped him from doing something. I think that he was stalking Elektra for some reason. He had eyes like a Dozal, you know what I mean? When they are stalking their prey that look, that dead look of total concentration on a single goal, to kill. He had that look. And we, I mean Dray, busted up his plans. He will want us to pay for that."

Harrison stood and stretched out his arms above his head. He was several inches taller than Gorski. His muscles were bulging as he flexed. "Sounds like one scary individual, Yuri. But you know, I have seen that look in your eyes before and you are not a killer. The one I am most worried for is Elektra. She is the youngest, the least experienced. Although I would imagine she has grown up considerably in the last few days."

"Yes, she has." Gorski was thinking of the lovely Greek girl. "She is lucky to be alive. Those men were intent on killing her. If Dray had not intervened, she would be dead."

Harrison's face changed expression, "You said she might have killed a man. I know what that is like. She, she will be going through nightmares, the emotional stress. I still see the look in his eyes, Yuri."

Gorski shook his head. There had been a group of drunken construction workers a year ago at a local bar that gave the gang some trouble. Gorski, Harrison, Gillis, Evart, Love-Easter, Guevara, DuBravac, Lincoln, Steiner, Klaus Rhinehard, Frank Glenn and the Andolini brothers were also there for a night of fun. The fight was started by the construction employees. No one could recall why they started it, what had been said or not said to spark the melee. In the course of the violent struggle, one large man pulled a knife on Harrison and tried to stab him with it. During their personal scuffle, the man fell on his own knife. He bled out before medical attention could arrive. Since that date, Harrison had blamed himself for the man's death. The grief Harrison felt led to the drinking. Soon after, Julia Steiner broke off her relationship with him. The situation was emotionally draining on everyone.

"Drew, don't go there," Gorski said softly.

"The broadcast says the sand storm might turn our way," Harrison told him, changing the uncomfortable subject. Both men knew if the storm system turned toward Clovis City, they would go into Lock Down and possibly be confined for a day or two until the winds subsided. "We might have time to go lift some weights, do a light workout before class. Want to come along?"

"Let's go," Gorski said, throwing his black gym bag over his shoulder. A work out would help him think and a little sweat would help Harrison burn off the alcohol intake from last night's festivities.

The two men walked out of their dormitory room together. They were talking about one of their professors and an assignment regarding criminal investigation as they made their way down the long hallway. Neither Harrison nor Gorski noticed the man in the cadet uniform following them. Gorski was the first out the exit to the men's dormitory with Harrison behind him. Their shadow spoke into his collar.

"This is Red One. Target is on the move," Sergeant First Class Mark Lund spoke into his communication device that was sewn into the cuff of his shirt. Lund was in Military Intelligence, also referred to as MI, under Colonel Gorski and had been assigned the task of protecting his son, Yuri. Lund looked young for his thirty years of age. He had been assigned to escort dignitaries in the past as their body guard. Lund was used to these types of assignments, which was probably why Colonel Gorski selected him. Before transferring to the Military Intelligence branch, Lund had been an Army Ranger and had served in the Dinosaur War. Lund was awarded several medals for his past service. Colonel Gorski trusted Lund with this assignment, the main reason was that during the three years Lund was a squad leader and then later a platoon sergeant, he had never lost a soldier in combat. Lund had short blonde hair and blue eyes. He was originally from the southern part of Sweden and had several sisters. He left home at seventeen years old to join the Armed Forces and seek out adventure. He had served on two Battle Cruisers and on Planet Athena before being assigned to planet New Edinburgh.

Gorski and Harrison covered their faces from the blowing light purple sand. They could hear the roar of the distant wind that seemed to warn of an approaching doom. Although the conditions from the distant sand storm was making walking difficult, the climatologists had not yet declared it an emergency requiring Lock Down. The campus gymnasium was several hundred yards in the distance. Gorski and Harrison began running for the facility to get out of the way of the wind.

The Clovis Academy gymnasium was eight floors high; it contained a lower level with a swimming pool and hot tubs. The second level had the individual cadets' lockers, showers and rest rooms. The third level one would find the large free weight room and computerized treadmills for running or walking. Level four was where the fifteen professional sized basketball courts were located. Level five had weight machines, with approximately two thousand different computerized machines for chest, shoulder, back, abdominal, legs, buttocks, arms, and every other muscle isolation apparatus imaginable. Level six had the twenty hand-ball courts. Level seven had fifteen tennis courts. Level eight was where the aerobic rooms and stationary computerized bicycles and stair machines were located. There was also a basement in which there were offices for the employees, cleaning crews, washing machines and dryers and supplies. Every level had stairs leading up and down. The floors were made out of pressurized crystal and a transparent metal found on Sikorsky's Planet. It was a hybrid creation that could withstand several tons of weight and was almost impossible to break. The cadets preferred the ability to see everything above or below them, making the gymnasium was also a good place to meet new people and find potential sex partners.

Gorski and Harrison entered the massive structure and walked past the large swimming pool. They both noticed that three of Marco and Dominic Andolini's younger sisters were jumping off the Olympic size diving boards into the water. The Andolini girls were all seventeen years old and absolutely beautiful. Gorski noticed that there were many men watching the three Andolini girls in their tiny bikinis. Gorski smiled to himself and kept walking toward the men's lockers to get changed into his gym sweats. Gorski felt sorry for any man that tried to mess with the Andolini girls. Their brothers Dominic and Marco would make their lives miserable.

There were several groups playing pick-up games of basketball on the fourth level. Some were one on one, others five against five. Basketball was encouraged due to the cardiovascular value of running, the muscle tone rewards gained from running, stopping and jumping and the hand eye coordination for dribbling, stealing and shooting the ball.

Gorski and Harrison dressed into their sweats and did not notice that Mark Lund and another were following them.

Jurgen Doernitz had showered with Melissa Harcourt and they had kissed goodbye. Doernitz promised he would return after class so they could spend more time together. Melissa sat on her bed after the younger man left her room. She began thinking that sleeping with Doernitz had been a mistake. She was accustomed to men coming to her bed and leaving. She preferred things that way. No promises needed to be made or kept. No hurt feelings and no emotional entanglements.

The problem with Doernitz was that he was far too nice, kind and caring. He was different from the other men she had been involved with. Melissa decided she needed to let him go now before she really hurt the man. Clearly, Doernitz was mistaking her physical affection for more and she did not want more at least not at this stage of her life.

Doernitz was stunned by the powerful winds as he left the women's dormitory building. He had never been exposed to one of New Edinburgh's infamous sand storms. The cadet ran toward the engineering lecture building for class. He covered his face as sand was thrown about. He prayed that the storm would pass by Clovis City.

Dean Golden Harvard looked at his digital clock time on his desk. It was almost ten a.m. and he was already exhausted. He was not accustomed to clandestine meetings before five a.m. He had met with his top staff to produce a list of cadets to compete in the annual Tournament, he had "enrolled" five fake cadets that were to be protection for five actual students and now, the threat of a dust storm sweeping in had his attention. Harvard had contacted the Clovis City climatologist experts and they told the Dean that they were deeply concerned that the storm could turn their direction. But it was still too early to predict. Playing it safe, Harvard contacted his multiple wives and instructed them to round up all of their children and get them to shelter. One of his wives did not respond to his attempt to reach her on his holo-com.

Priscilla Danton Harvard was born and raised on planet New Berlin. She had never left her home planet until the day she had been married off to Golden Harvard by her family. The details of the contractual agreement were unknown to the bride. Priscilla Danton had just turned eighteen years old at the time of the arranged ceremony. Her husband was much older than she was and already had numerous wives and too many children for her to keep track of. When she heard her holo-com device vibrating she did not answer as she was somewhere she should not be. She was at a seedy hotel room with a student of her husband's Academy. She moaned pleasurably as Rolf Rhinehard made love to her on the floor of the cheap hotel room. They had been involved in an affair for months, both knowing that if caught, Rolf would lose his position at the Academy by expulsion. Rolf preferred the companionship of married women since those relationships insulated him from the inevitable desires for long term commitments. Rolf enjoyed his freedom to do as he pleased and having relationships with married women allowed for that. He could have all the sex he needed with no commitments to burden him.

Rolf did not hear the buzzing sound of her holo-com. All he heard was the sounds of their passion, the moans of the woman and the wail of the winds outside the hotel room.

After considerable grief over the loss of Drayton, Les Gillis decided he needed to see an old friend. He dressed in a pair of old black jeans, a grey sweatshirt with the Clovis Academy logo emblazoned in red and a black leather biker jacket given to him a few years ago by an old girlfriend. He had his face covered with a thick scarf and goggles for his eyes due to the sand and the winds. He quickly exited the men's dormitory building and was met with the stiff winds. He walked in the direction of the married cadets homes which was approximately one kilometer distance from the cadet buildings. He had not contacted Yesenia Guevara due to her husband being the jealous type. The bigger excuse was that William Bragg was the leader of the gang named after his family. Bragg, along with his little brother and about three dozen malcontents terrorized the younger cadets. They were always picking fights and looking for trouble. The Bragg group hazed the other cadets without remorse and would even steal their personal property. Gillis, along with Yuri Gorski and their group had gotten the best of the William Bragg Gang on several occasions.

Gillis knew Yesenia Guevara's husband was in class at the time and most likely she would be home alone. He watched many other cadets running to find cover due to the high winds. He picked up his pace, moving faster. Although Yesenia had married a rival of Drayton Love-Easter, Gillis was understanding of her situation. If she had not married someone, the government of the Glorious Leader would have taken her son and put him up for adoption. Guevara did what she had to do to keep her child, which was to marry a man she did not actually love.

The home of Yesenia Guevara and William Bragg was the same as the home of Porfirio and Freya Cardenas. All of the living quarters for the married cadets were designed exactly the same. When he arrived at the doorstep, Gillis pressed the keyboard at the door. He heard her voice.

"Yes?"

"Yesenia, it's me Les. I wanted to speak with you," Gillis said as he was dusting himself off.

"Door is open. Come in."

Gillis walked into the home as the doors slid open for him. There was a wedding picture of the lovely Guevara and William Bragg on the left wall from the doorway. There were pictures of her son, Joseph, on the wall to the right. The living area was nice, with a white couch, love seat and light blue tiled floors. Gillis heard the automatic door slide shut behind him. Guevara walked from out of the kitchen. She was wearing a bright yellow half shirt and white shorts. She still had the long dark hair that first caught Love-Easter's attention years earlier. Her light brown skin and a pretty smile that were enough to turn any man's head.

She hugged Gillis tight. She was happy that he had thought enough of her to stop by. After learning of Love-Easter's murder, her husband had become intolerable in the way that he reveled in the tragedy. The sad truth was that her heart had always belonged to Love-Easter and she was forced to grieve in silence. "It has been too long Les."

"Yes it has. We have all really missed you."

"Please, have a seat. I was just cleaning in the kitchen," she told him. Gillis loved her accent. Guevara had been born in Columbia, South

America and was the daughter of a space ship pilot. She had numerous siblings as her father took on several wives and had followed the direction of the Glorious Leader by taking the strong fertility drugs that were available to the public like candy was for children during Halloween. "Would you like some tea or coffee? I just brewed a fresh pot."

"Yes, coffee would be nice," Gillis told her as he sat down.

Guevara had been one of the original Gorski Gang members. For about two years she and Drayton Love-Easter were always together as lovers. Gillis, as Love-Easter's roommate, knew the two had considered marriage. But one day Love-East made a serious mistake. Melissa Harcourt had set her sights on him and she used her mental powers and her seductive scents to lure Love-Easter into a sexual frenzy. Guevara walked into the dormitory room and caught the two in bed together. The relationship was over and Guevara left the group. Love-Easter tried to win her back on several occasions, but Guevara could not forgive him.

She walked out of the kitchen with two coffee cups in her hands. She handed one of the cups to Gillis and sat down next to him on the couch. He took a drink of the coffee.

"That is perfect," Gillis smiled at her. He then noticed the bruises on her arms and her left cheek. His face flushed with anger. "What the hell?"

Guevara turned her face away in shame, "It was my fault. I caused him to lose his temper." She pulled her long hair down over her cheek in an attempt to cover the bruise.

It was well known that William Bragg had problems controlling his anger. Bragg had moved in on Guevara when she stopped seeing Love-Easter. Guevara married Bragg for one reason and that was because she was pregnant and did not want to be a single mother. Bragg, in his efforts to win her over, claimed he did not care that she was pregnant with another man's child. He was insistent that he would raise the child as his own. He married her after she had given birth to her son, Joseph Guevara Bragg. Her first beating came when she had suggested that the child should have the Love-Easter name.

"I will kill him!" Gillis jumped to his feet in anger. Gillis had been raised that no man should treat a woman with such disrespect or brutality. His hands were balled up into fists.

"No, please, Les!" Guevara pleaded as she covered her face with her hands. "Will was upset. When I heard about Drayton yesterday, I was crying and I couldn't stop. Will knew I had never stopped loving Dray. I deserved this. He had every right to be angry with me."

The bruises on the arm looked like finger prints, from grabbing the woman too tightly. The cheek bruise was clearly from Bragg slapping or hitting her.

Gillis was furious; his entire face was red with anger. Guevara had been one of his closest friends over the last three years and she was a good and decent person that never did anything to harm another.

"You did not deserve it! He has no right to harm you. I am going to speak with him about this!" Gillis promised as he clenched his fists.

Guevara was still pleading, "Please, Les. If you say anything to him he will know that you were here with me. He will accuse me of sleeping with you or something. It will only set him off again. Please do not say anything to him."

"If you forbid me to speak with him, then I will turn him in to law enforcement. Family violence assaults are felonies under the Clovis City Charter Laws," Gillis reminded her. "He should be prosecuted. You did nothing to deserve this. Bragg is an animal, Yesenia. You need to get your son and get away from him. There is no telling what he is capable of. Besides that, you know that he spends time at the dorm room of several of the Lipinski sisters. It is common knowledge around the Academy that he is sleeping with half of them. You do not deserve to live with a man that beats you and then cheats on you with multiple lovers. Please, Yesenia. Please let me help you pack up and move out."

Guevara began crying. Her emotions were out of her control since she was stuck in an abusive marriage to a man she did not love while the man she had truly loved had been murdered. She had been systematically alienated from all of her friends. Bragg prohibited her from contacting anyone. If she made any attempt at reaching out to another, Bragg would physically assault her. She wanted to change the subject matter of their conversation, even though she knew that Gillis was correct about Bragg. "Les, I have been so upset. Were you there when he died?"

Gillis hugged her and allowed her to cry on his shoulder, "Yes I was there. Yesenia, he was unconscious when they killed him. He did not suffer."

"I sometimes would think, would my life be better had I given him a second chance. I just could not forgive what he did. It hurt me so much to see him with that other woman." She was sobbing as she spoke.

Gillis told her not to worry about such things. Melissa Harcourt had no boundaries when it came to relationships. If she wanted to be with a man, she just took him and the consequences be damned. Love-Easter never lost the feelings of remorse for his betrayal of Guevara. As his best friend, Gillis knew that Love-Easter's biggest regret was that he had caused her so much pain.

Gillis and Guevara sat together for what seemed hours, holding each other and letting the tears flow. Gillis knew he had made the right decision by coming to see her. They both needed to share their mutual grief. They had been the two closest people to Drayton Love-Easter in the Academy.

Gillis decided he was going to make sure William Bragg never laid a hand on Guevara again. He owed it to her and to Drayton.

After some time, the two friends continued to drink their coffee.

"Will you ever tell your son about his true father?" Gillis asked.

Guevara was wiping the tears from her cheeks as she smiled and nodded, "One day, yes. When he is older. I want Drayton's son to know about him. Can you imagine when he is old enough, contacting his "preacher of family values" grandfather and telling him 'Hi, I am your illegitimate grand-child'?"

They both laughed at that thought. They hugged again.

Guevara had given much thought to the difficulty of telling her son that the man he grew up believing to be his father was not really the biological father. Guevara was thankful that the day she would have that conversation with her son was many years in the future.

Outside the home, Corporal Frank Preston, Gillis' body guard waited. The sand storm was getting worse. Preston had to cover his face with a hood and put goggles over his eyes. Preston was an Army Ranger that was serving in the Military Intelligence unit at the Clovis City United Nations Command under Colonel Gorski. If the storm worsened, he would have no choice but to reveal himself to Gillis. After a while, Preston decided it was time to check in.

"This is Red Three," he spoke into his small holo-com to report in to his co-workers. "Target is in a secure location. If the Dust Storm gets too strong, we may have to think up a new strategy."

Preston was twenty years old from a family with a history of military service. He had aspired to become an officer but at some point elected to join the enlisted ranks. He was a better than average marksman and qualified black belt in karate. His best asset was in self-defense. He looked young and could pass for a teen if he needed to, which was probably why Lund and Colonel Gorski selected him for the task.

Jen Staszko joined Yuri Gorski and Drew Harrison at the campus gymnasium. She wanted to release the stress of the past few days as did the two men. After she hugged Harrison and laid a big kiss on Gorski,

Staszko made her way to the treadmill machines. At each of her workouts, Staszko started off with either some aerobic program or a five mile run. Gorski and Harrison immediately went to the free weight room and started stretching their muscles.

Staszko noticed that there was a man and a woman in the gym that seemed to be following them. She slowly pulled out her five inch long holo-com device so that the two people trailing her would not notice. She could not see Gorski or Harrison from the treadmill room as the free weight room was in a different area. "Computer, person to person. Yuri Gorski."

Gorski was spotting Drew Harrison on the bench press. They had started off by warming up with two hundred pounds, Harrison was lifting the bar bell with the weights when Gorski's holo-com device began buzzing. Harrison replaced the bar bell on the bench press rest when he realized his spotter had to take an incoming call. Safety was always first when lifting weights.

"This is Yuri," Gorski answered.

"Baby, it's me. There is some strange man and woman here. I think they have been following us ever since we left the dorms," Staszko reported.

"Be right there," Gorski said and motioned with his head to Harrison.   The two men moved quickly to the treadmill room. They spied upon the two strangers Staszko had alerted them to. There were other cadets and professors working out, but Gorski had seen all of them before. These two were out of their element. The man was blonde with blue eyes and seemed to be in excellent physical condition. The woman was black skinned with curly dark hair and light brown eyes. She was exotic looking with a toned body and attractive face.

Bold as always, Gorski quickly approached them.

The man and woman seemed startled when Gorski was standing before them. Harrison and Staszko were on opposite sides of Gorski, forming a triangle around the two strangers.

"Can I help you?" Sergeant First Class Mark Lund asked, trying to sound natural and cover up his surprise. In his mind he was thinking, not good. They spotted us too quickly.

"Who are you?" Gorski demanded. "Why are you following us?"

"Because your father ordered us to do so," Lund answered calmly. "I am Mark Lund and this is LaShondra Lewis. We were ordered to keep an eye on you two."

"Really?" Harrison said skeptically as he looked over LaShondra Lewis. He immediately found the woman attractive and smiled at her. To his surprise she smiled back.

"Yes," Lund nodded. "Now that we have met, why don't we all work out together? That way your fellow students will get used to us being around you."

"There were supposed to be five of you," Gorski said suspiciously.

"And the other three are watching their assigned person," LaShondra Lewis assured them. She extended her right hand and waited for the cadets to shake. "But for now, Jen Staszko, I am your new best friend."

Lewis had been born and raised in Alabama Territory of Old Earth. She had been runner up as Prom Queen at her local school and had been popular with her classmates. Her parents had been elementary school teachers and were disappointed when their daughter rejected a college education to join the military service. Lewis wanted to see the universe and the quickest and most economical way to travel throughout the solar systems was in the Marines. She signed up as a volunteer upon her graduation from high school. In the last two years, Lewis had seen three solar systems and two space stations. For the past few months she had been serving as a Marine Corps Corporal. Lewis was twenty years old, single and had no children.

Staszko smiled and reached out with her hand and grasped the hand that Lewis had offered. The women shook hands and Staszko found that Lewis had a tight grip. "Pleased to meet you, new best friend." Staszko sized Lewis up in the few seconds she observed her. She determined Lewis was a woman that could handle herself in a combat situation.

"So, I was watching you start up your work out. Two hundred pounds? Is that the best you can do?" Lund challenged Gorski and Harrison.

"I can do much more," Harrison was insulted by the question.

Lund reached out and grabbed Harrison's bulging arm. "With

triceps and biceps like these, you should be doing double that amount."

"Well, Mark, you want to join us?" Gorski wanted to see what the man was made of.

Lund smiled, pointing in the direction of the free weight room. "Gentlemen, let's go get some work in."

"Let's go," Gorski led the group over. The five found that they had one thing in common; they all enjoyed a solid session of working out. During the hour and a half that they spent together, they became friends. Or, as Lewis had stated, new best friends.

Jack Harcourt and Michel Evart had been amateur basketball players since their middle school days and enjoyed competing in pick-up games at the gymnasium. The two cadets would join many other cadets on the courts and select team mates and attempt to defeat the opposite team. Evart noticed a tall white male approaching them bearing a wide smile on his face. The man was in black shorts and a sleeveless jersey.

The man seemed to be sizing up Evart and Harcourt. "Hey, you two up for a game? We need two more to finish out the second team?"

"Yeah, we would like to join in," Harcourt nodded to the stranger. He wondered why he had never seen the tall man before. "Are you a student at the Academy?"

"Yes sir. My name is Bill."

"I'm Michel, he's Jack." Evart shook the cadet's hand while introducing himself and Harcourt. "We're both cadet pilots. How about you?"

"The same," the cadet named Bill led Harcourt and Evart across the basketball court to the farthest court on the floor.

Evart noticed that pre-medical student Clark Blundell was stretching next to a botany major named Li Mingjuan. Evart knew that the two cadets had been something of an item around campus. Evart and Harcourt had played pick-up basketball against Blundell and Mingjuan in the past. They nodded at each other and smiled.

The man named Bill pointed to the court, "So, are we going to shoot some hoops are what?"

Evart watched the new cadet named Bill join Blundell and Mingjuan on the court with Lin Xiaojun, who was studying for his doctorate in stellar seismology and Roy Starr who was a cadet pilot and full-fledged member of the infamous Bragg Gang. Starr scowled at Evart and Harcourt but said nothing.

Evart and Harcourt joined three other cadets on the court and began to pick their positions on their team. Harcourt was wearing black shorts and an orange, sleeveless t-shirt. He was chosen to be the point guard for his team of five players. Reynita Calderon was wearing a white half shirt and white shorts. She was selected to play shooting guard. Evart was grateful to have her on his team as her shots from the three point line were almost always perfect. Blundell was their small forward. Evart was wearing the same colors as Harcourt and was playing the power forward position. The fifth team member was a hydraulic engineering student that was seven feet tall named Hua Thon Ye he was selected to play the center position.

The opposing team had the new cadet named Bill playing at center. As the competition progressed, he proved to be a rebounding machine. Neither Harcourt nor Evart had seen the tall cadet before that day. Evart was clearly getting frustrated when the tall opponent kept blocking all of his shots. Hua Thon Ye experienced the same frustration against the tall newcomer. They had been playing non-stop for about thirty minutes straight before all of the men and women playing agreed to take a ten minute break. Reynita Calderon had been the high scorer for both teams, hitting four straight shots from beyond the three point line. Harcourt and Evart grabbed some towels and ran down the two flights of stairs to the huge free weight room to meet with their other friends.

They had noticed that Gorski, Staszko and Harrison were in the free weights room before they joined the pick-up game started. They met Gorski, Harrison, Stasko and two others as they were working on bench presses and incline presses.

Hugs were exchanged. Harcourt was grateful to see his friends alive and well. They exchanged introductions with the two new cadets.

The new cadet from the basketball pick-up game had joined the group. Mark Lund waived the tall man over and introduced him to the others. "This is Bill Hodges. He is Michel's shadow."

Hodges shook hands with each of the cadets. He was already well acquainted with Lund and Lewis from their military service as fellow MI platoon members. Hodges was a few inches shy of seven feet tall. He had been giving Evart and Harcourt's team hell on the basketball court.

"So, you are supposed to be protecting me?" Evart asked him, still breathing heavily.

"Those are my orders," Hodges said.

"Good, then when we go back upstairs, you are on our team." Evart shook his hand. "He is single handedly kicking our ass upstairs. I never saw someone that could rebound and block shots so effortlessly. Where did you learn to play ball so well?"

Hodges shrugged, "I was a scholarship recipient from Texas University three years ago. I blew my knee out in my freshmen year so I joined the military. I wanted to see the galaxy and all that. But I still play in pick-up games like yours, to keep my skills sharp."

"Man, you can play on our team any day," Harcourt was still breathing hard.

The other basketball players were yelling down stairs at Harcourt, Evart and Hodges to rejoin them. Break time was over. The three men ran back up the stair case to finish their friendly competition. Hodges joined his team and they began to set up for the inbound pass from Harcourt's team. Hodges smiled at Reynita and she returned the gesture. Hodges liked the fact that the woman was a very talented outside shooter. Hodges observed that she played pretty good defense as well.

Lund asked Staszko and Harrison to get closer to him and Lewis. "Look, I want us to all stay together yet be separate at the same time. If we all congregate at the same building, a smart bomb will be the end of us all.

Corporal Lewis and I have formulated a plan that will be perfect, if the lock down is announced due to that approaching dust storm. We will need to keep some of you in the men's dormitory, some in the women's and one in another location. Now, we do not know how many will come at us or when. But those are some things we cannot control. But we will control what we can."

"Such as?" Staszko asked as she was adjusting her weight lifting gloves.

"First, you all need to be in locations where there is more than one exit," Lund told them. "Secondly, we need to designate a location that we can all meet if we happen to be separated. It needs to be a place well-guarded and where civilians normally do not frequent."

"The Protective Walls," Gorski suggested. "The fifty foot brick and metal walls all around Clovis City. Civilians avoid it due to the proximity of the jungle and the ease in which a Cawler can swoop down and snatch a person. But for us it could be perfect. There are Marine Corps guards all over the wall, watching for Tree Spiders, Cawlers, Verburgt, and other dangers. We could plan on a rendezvous point on the top level of the wall."

"I like that idea," Lewis said, nodding thoughtfully.

"Alright, the Protective Wall," Lund agreed. "Say marker thirteen, just near the large gold statue of the Glorious Leader. That is pretty much directly behind the men's dormitory and only a three kilometer run to reach it." The fifty foot high Protective Wall was marked off on the bottom by each kilometer of distance. Thus, marker thirteen would be the number the cadets would seek out to meet.

"And third?" Gorski asked.

"Third, you cadets stick to your body guard unless we instruct you to run," Lund said gravely. "If we tell you to run do not hesitate. Do not stay and try to help us. If we instruct you to get away, then it means we are in deep trouble."

The pick-up basketball game came to a close soon after a near riot at the public pool had ended. Evart and Harcourt told Hodges that their plan was to shower and then get back over to the dormitory.

"Okay, then we will shower and get over there," Hodges nodded as he checked his holo-com device for the weather report. "I think the sand storm is coming our way."

Jack Harcourt had noticed the body language between Calderon and Hodges during the game. Although the Calderon's were members of the Bragg Gang, Reynita always seemed to be nice to the Gorski group. Harcourt pointed in the direction of Reynita. She was using a large white towel to wipe the sweat off her face and arms.

"Bill, we just met and I normally don't give strangers any advice," Harcourt began, "But Reynita over there seems to really like you. You might want to take a few seconds to, you know, talk to her."

"I'm on duty," Hodges sighed as he looked over at Calderon.

"I can watch Michel for a few minutes," Harcourt smiled at him. "I am a child of Athena and could use some of my gifts to hold off any attack.

"Go get the girl," Evart pat Hodges on the back. "Live a little. Jack can protect me."

Hodges watched as Reynita smiled at his direction. He wanted to go and talk to the attractive sharp shooting guard but his concept of duty did not allow him to do so. He smiled back at her, waived good-bye and walked toward the men's showers.

Calderon watched the new cadet walk away with Evart and Harcourt. She looked down at the ground with disappointment before slowly walking toward the women's showers. She really found the new cadet to be handsome and thought he found her to be attractive as well. At least it seemed that way when she would catch him checking her out. She wondered what was wrong with her. She never could keep a man interested in her for very long. And this tall man that was such a fantastic basketball player seemed interested but he did not act on it. Calderon decided she should go home to her parents and wait out the storm. Perhaps another day the new cadet would want to spend some time with her.

CHAPTER SEVEN

Astronaut Lieutenant Aura Lynda Glenn received her orders to command a weather research Raumschiff to scan the out of control dust storm. She had been newly promoted from Lieutenant Junior Grade and assigned her own squadron of forty-two pilots in Dakota Province of planet New Edinburgh. Glenn notified the climatologists that were to fly with her that the mission would lift off in fifteen minutes. She gathered her flight suit and ran toward the long Planetary Defense landing strip which housed one hundred Raumschiffs and one thousand Allen Type Fighter ships.

Glenn boarded the three level space ship from the rear loading ramp and rushed past two engineers, three MI soldiers and two computer technicians on her way to the upper level. She found that the three seats in the pilot section were empty. She sat down in the pilot chair and began her security checks as she had learned in the Academy under Admiral Seward. As she continued her work to determine whether the ship was safe for flight, she multi-tasked by firing up the rear engines and began plotting her flight path. Once she was informed that the team of climatologists was on board, she ordered that the rear ramp be retracted and the hull sealed.

She cleared the ship for lift off with the space traffic controllers and then guided the ship up into the sky. She steered the ship into the direction of the dust storm that was veering violently in the direction of Lynott's Land. Within half an hour, she could see the whirlwind that resembled an upside down tornado. It was spewing purple sand in every direction and Glenn had to quickly react by jolting the steering column several time to avoid a large tree that had been ripped from the ground. She hoped the crew members had secured their safety belts each time she had to dodge one of the trees that had been turned into a projectile.

The climatologists did their scans on the storm and came to a shocking conclusion. The eye of the storm was shifting in the direction of Clovis City. Glenn immediately informed the Planetary Defense of the findings.

The alarms in Clovis City began to sound simultaneously. Loud klaxons alerted the citizens, visitors, tourists, soldiers and students of the massive walled in city that the Dust Storm was starting to move in their direction. "Warning! In one hour, all protective barricades will lower over each building and the flight hangers. Warning! Once the barricades have lowered they will not reopen and you will be left to face the storm." The warnings repeated themselves across the entire city.

Citizens and military personnel began moving for the cover of buildings to avoid being trapped out in the open. People were also working to get their livestock of poggie's, horses, cats and other pets indoors before the carnage arrived. The chances of surviving a sand storm on planet New Edinburgh were very good if shelter was obtained. Any person exposed to the elements would be dead for certain.

Cadet William Bragg heard the alarms ringing outside his cheap hotel room. He used the room about three times a week to bring some random female cadet over for a session of sex. Due to the frequency that he would use the hotel, the owner gave him a discount on the normal room price. He sat up and looked for his clothes, cursing his bad luck. He was in the middle of making love to one of his many sex partners, Natusia Lipinski, when the annoying sirens began. The two were naked and things had been getting interesting on the queen size bed they had been lying on, smothering each other with kisses filled with lust. He hated leaving the woman without finishing what they had started.

"You're leaving?" Natusia asked him with surprise in her voice.

"Sorry, babe. But you know that I am married so I have to get home before the Lock Down. You should get back to your dorm room while you can." Bragg found his socks on the floor and pulled them over his feet.

"Why keep going back to her, Will? You don't even love her. Why?" The disappointment in her voice was evident.

Natusia was a lovely girl that had about four dozen sisters; almost all of them were in the Academy and loyal Bragg Gang members. Bragg enjoyed sleeping with the Lipinski sisters as they each had athletic, slender bodies and were generous lovers in the bedroom. He had been sexually active with five of the sisters off and on for the past year and would flaunt the fact that he was having multiple affairs to anyone that cared to listen. He made it a habit to tell his wife each time he played hide the chorizo with another woman which would spark an argument and gave Bragg the excuse to beat her. He found pleasure in hitting Yesenia Guevara and looked for new and innovative ways to cause her physical harm. Natusia was correct, he had not married Yesenia for love. He married her to beat her and through each beating he gained some feeling of revenge against Drayton Love-Easter from the accursed Gorski Gang. Bragg was cognizant that his views were twisted and even demented to an extent. He simply did not care.

"You are right that I do not love her, but that is not the point. She is my property and I can do with her as I wish."

Natusia pulled her purple Clovis Academy t-shirt over her head as he spoke. Although she enjoyed having sex with Bragg, she found him to be a cruel man. He had hurt just about every woman he ever came in contact with. His marriage to Yesenia Guevara was a sham, everyone on campus knew that fact, and those that did not know were the students that Bragg had not yet told.

"You could have me or one of my sisters, Bill, anytime. Reynita really liked you, too. One of us could make you happy. Just leave Yesenia already and get on with your life."

Bragg pulled on his cadet uniform and zipped it up. He glared at Natusia for a few seconds as he considered her words. "Happy? Who gives a shit about happy? I do what I wish to do when I wish to do it. She is mine to torture, beat and torment and I will do it because I wish to. Now, get your lovely ass back to the dorms. I am going home to beat my wife."

The truth that Bragg dared not admit to was that he could not bring himself to start a serious relationship with any of the Lipinski sisters or Reynita. The Lipinski's had strong ties to the community and he would not be able to isolate any of them effectively from their large extended family. Reynita Calderon had a close knit family as well as many friends. Any man that attempted to slap or hit Reynita would have all of her headstrong brothers out for blood. Bragg liked women that he could control completely. He could get away with his abuse of Yesenia Guevara. But he would never be able to hide his activities with either a Lipinski girl or Reynita.

Junior Ragnarsson received the information regarding the storm as he was sitting in his Raumschiff next to his sister Emma. His assassination team nodded in unison as each of them understood what a gift nature was giving to them. This was what they had hoped for. The storm would cover their tracks, there would be no civilian interventions and the military guards would be under cover and therefore useless to the cadets. The five targets would be on their own, trapped in their dormitories and defenseless.

Junior had ordered that each of his team dress up as if they were students at the Academy. The men had on long sleeved and long legged sweats that had several zipper pockets on the chest, sleeves and sides of the legs. Inside those pockets were laser pistols, knives, stun darts and other weapons that the hit team intended to use against the five cadets. Emma and Dulce were clad in long sleeved jump suits that had numerous pockets that were filled with similar weaponry.

The team had read the dossiers of the five cadet targets and of their closest friends. There were no illusions as to the challenge. Junior had already instructed the team to stun Dominic Andolini and Jack Harcourt on sight, Harcourt because he was a Child of Athena and Dominic because of his marksmanship scores.

"Listen up!" Junior yelled to the team. "My father instructed that we only take the five cadets prisoner. He prefers we bring them back to Rosenburg's Ranch to be fed to the pets at the Arena. Stun any cadet that gets in your way. No killing of collaterals. My father wants this clean. Only kill the targets if necessary."

"Our little brother Ivar is waiting for us at the landing strip," Emma told them. She needed for the mission to be a success to cover for her previous failure. Her father would not be kind to her if the cadets escaped them a second time. "I will go with Dulce and Ivar to the Women's Dormitory. The rest of you will go to the men's. We meet back here on the Raumschiff in three hours. Regardless of the weather, we lift off at that time. Understood?"

The five trained killers nodded their heads. Nikko was sharpening one of his knives as Emma spoke to them, saying nothing.

Junior felt compelled to give his team one last instruction, "Remember the information that you each read. Gorski has a Harcourt in his corner. If you encounter the Harcourt, stun him or stun dart him. Do not give him the opportunity to use his mental mind control powers. Also remember his friend Dominic Andolini is an expert sniper. If Andolini gets his hands on a laser, a knife or any other weapon he can exact damage on us. If we get into a conflict with Gorski and his people, make Dominic Andolini and Jack Harcourt your first priorities. Drop them both."

They could feel the force of the winds rocking the space craft. The team members began pocketing stun darts, hand and leg binders. Prescott was disappointed he would not get to strangle someone on this mission. He loved it when a victim would kick and struggle as he choked the life out of them. Prescott hoped that some idiot would resist so he could use that as his excuse to kill.

Les Gillis was still talking with Yesenia Guevara when the warning alarms began to sound. Guevara's eyes widened with fear.

"You had best return to the dormitory," she told him. "William will be on his way back here. If he sees you, there might be trouble."

"No worries, Yesenia. I will get going. If he lays a hand on you again I will come and I will kick his damn ass to hell and back." Gillis stood up and turned to the hallway leading to the doorway as he heard the double metallic doors sliding open.

To their mutual surprise, William Bragg walked in at that moment through the opening provided by the front sliding doors. He was wearing his one-piece light blue cadet uniform that was covered with purple sand. Bragg paused, looking at the two and glared at his wife and then regarded Gillis. Other than the howl of the fierce winds outside, there was silence in the room. Gillis stared back at Bragg and the tension from the intensity in the eyes of the two men grew with each passing second. His face seemed to indicate that he was surprised that Gillis would have the audacity to be in his home. Confrontation between them seemed to be inevitable.

Bragg was a part of a large sibling group on New Edinburgh, his father was a mechanical engineer and his mothers were all in the medical field. He was a weight lifter and spent all of his spare time working on his chiseled body, compensating each workout with steroids which added bulk to his frame. Bragg was a cadet senior studying weapons and security with a goal to join either the Marines or Military Intelligence after graduation. He had short dark hair and was slightly taller than Gillis.

Bragg's face went from the look of surprise to rage.

"What the hell are you doing here?" Bragg demanded.

"It is great to see you again, too, Will," Gillis said calmly with hopes that he could diffuse the situation. "I came by to see my old friends. How are you doing these days, Will?"

"Cut the crap!" Bragg pointed his right index finger at Gillis and then at Guevara. "You are screwing my wife, aren't you?"

So much for defusing the situation, Gillis thought to himself.

"Will, I would never do that to you and she would not either. You know better than that."

"Ha! You expect me to believe that? You have been itching for a way to get back at me for stealing Reynita away from you! So this is how you are going to get your revenge, by sleeping with my woman?" Bragg dropped his gymnasium bag he had been carrying over his shoulder.

"Please, Bill! Les is telling the truth!" Guevara told him.

"I'll deal with you later, bitch! Let's go Gillis! You and me!" Bragg's eyes were darting back and forth like a wild man as he snarled his words.

The anger in Bragg had been building for many months. The fact that Guevara and Gillis were close friends was well known to him. That relationship was contrary to Bragg's efforts to isolate Guevara from all of her friends. Early in their marriage, Bragg had forced Guevara to avoid sitting with her old friends in the cafeteria. He did not allow her to speak with any of her girlfriends on her holo-com and had confiscated the device from her. Bragg had forced her to no longer sit next to her friends in the lecture halls at the Academy. Bragg had even killed Guevara's pet cat in order to keep her in line.

Even with all of his efforts to isolate her, Les Gillis, one of Guevara's oldest friends, was in his home, sitting on his couch. His very presence was a threat to Bragg's campaign to isolate Guevara. Bragg had decided that Les Gillis had to be punished.

"Apologize to the lady," Gillis said calmly.

Bragg spit on his own floor. "After I gut you, I am going to knock that bitch into next week! Outside! Now!"

"You first," Gillis motioned toward the door. Enough was enough. Gillis decided that Bragg needed a good ass kicking.

Bragg walked to the door, stomping his feet as he walked.

"Will, please!" Guevara was pleading. "Nothing is happening! We are only friends. Please. Stop this!"

Gillis followed behind the abusive man and watched as the door slid open for Bragg. Gillis walked outside and felt the power of the rapid winds. Bragg had his fists curled and quickly threw a right arm punch at Gillis. Gillis ducked under the swing and hit Bragg's ribs on his right side. Bragg yelled out as Gillis followed by hitting Bragg on the back of his neck with his left fist. Bragg fell and rolled onto the paved walkway. He rolled away from Gillis and was wiping purple sand from his mouth and away from his eyes.

Gillis stood facing Bragg, ready. Bragg charged his opponent and tried to tackle him. Gillis stepped to his left and Bragg snarled with rage when he could not grasp him. Gillis knew that Bragg was much stronger than he was which meant he could not allow the man to grab him. Bragg charged again, growling. Gillis dodged him and hit Bragg on the left side of his jaw as he attempted to run past him. Bragg fell to the ground screaming with rage. Gillis could hear Guevara yelling for the men to stop. Gillis was bouncing up and down on the balls of his feet, watching through the whirling sand as Bragg approached much slower this time.

Gillis waited and delivered a crescent kick into Bragg's massive chest. Bragg grunted and fell backwards to the ground. He jumped to his feet, screaming that he was going to kill Gillis. Bragg ran at Gillis, swinging wildly at him. Gillis jumped to the left, but one of Bragg's swings caught him on his right shoulder. Gillis rolled to the ground from the force of the hit. As Gillis rolled, Bragg was on him, tackling him to the ground. Gillis found himself pinned to the pavement as Bragg began hitting Gillis in his face and body. Gillis struggled to get loose of his grip. Bragg was stronger and kept hitting him with his right fist and holding him in place with his left arm and legs. Gillis gave a few good punches to Bragg's face, but Gillis was receiving the worst of it.

Gillis was surprised when Bragg was lifted off of him by a stranger. Bragg was cussing and yelling at the new man that had come to aid Gillis in the fight. Gillis struggled to stand back on his feet. The other man had strapped restraints on Bragg's wrists.

"Calm down!" The man was telling Bragg. "The fight is over!"

"Screw yourself!" Bragg screamed and charged head first at the stranger. Gillis reached out with his right leg and tripped Bragg, causing him to fall face first into the pavement. He was out cold.

"Thanks for the assist!" Gillis yelled to the stranger over the roar of the wind. "Who are you?"

"I am your shadow. Corporal Frank Preston at your service," he shook Gillis' hand. The two men watched Guevara help her abusive husband sit up.   "I think we need to get the two of you to medical, see if there are any broken bones," Preston suggested as he looked over the blood on Gillis' hands and face.

Gillis nodded, as his lip was bleeding and he could feel pain in his sides. Better safe than sorry and Bragg did not look good either. "Yeah. Let's get a transport shuttle and get to the ER before we go into Lock Down."

"Let me get my son!" Guevara yelled at them. "I am going with you."

A white Emergency Glider arrived within three minutes from the main hospital. The vehicle could ascend about thirty feet in the air and travel at speeds of two hundred kilometers an hour. It was able to transport about fifteen injured people at a time. It had a Red Cross symbol painted on the sides for identification purposes. The pilot landed in front of the Bragg/Guevara quarters as a nurse and a doctor jumped out of the back of the Glider and carried a rolling bed. The doctor and nurse lifted William Bragg onto the bed and rushed him to the Glider. Gillis, Preston and Guevara, holding her sleeping child in her arms, boarded the Glider. Within seconds, they were airborne.

Jen Staszko hated being separated from Yuri Gorski. Their body guards indicated that they needed to be placed in teams to draw out any would be assassins. When the group of cadets and undercover soldiers reached the crossroads of the men's and women's dormitory buildings, Gorski gave Staszko a long hug and kiss good-bye. Staszko did not want to let go of her man. They reluctantly parted and she watched with sad eyes as Gorski walked toward his dormitory building. Staszko could feel the strong winds hitting her, blowing her long hair across her face. She turned to walk into her building with LaShondra Lewis at her side.

"Are you in love with him?" Lewis asked loud enough for Staszko to hear over the winds.

Staszko covered her eyes with her hands as she walked and smiled, "Yes. A good man is hard to find and Yuri is one of the best. Any woman would love him."

The populace of Clovis City was in panic mode. People were running all over the streets back and forth, seeking out shelter from the storm. Yuri Gorski, Michel Evart, Drew Harrison, Jack Harcourt, Mark Lund and Bill Hodges rushed through crowds of people to get to the men's dormitory building. Pieces of shrubbery, paper, plastic and other light objects were blown about with ease by the powerful winds. Jen Staszko and LaShondra Lewis made their way to the women's dormitory. Soon, the barricades would lower.

Gorski regarded the men's dormitory. If a hit team makes it in, then the building would potentially be a death trap. There would be no escape during lock down. The metal barricade would lower from the roof to the ground and connect with large clamps which would protect the building from flying trees or other large objects. During the duration of the storm, no one would be able to get in or out.

The winds were howling and sounded like a train approaching. The sirens were wailing over the sound of the wind. Gorski followed everyone inside and hoped for the best.

The six men rushed up the stair case and to the level where Gorski and Harrison's room was located. Fortunately, Evart and Harcourt lived just a few rooms down the hallway. All six made it to Gorski's room and the door shut behind them. The large entryway to the dormitory was full of cadets yelling and shouting with excitement. For the vast majority of the students, this was their first experience with a dust storm. To the right of the main entrance was the massive student union game room area. Lund estimated that a few hundred men and women were settling in for a night of computer gaming, chess matches and card games. To the left was a small cafeteria that was full of cadets eating sandwiches or soups, which were the only two main menu items.

Lund had developed a plan in case there was an attempt on the lives of the cadets. They would put traps on the individual doors to alert if any person entered the room and have hidden cameras to film the interior of each room. Each of the team would take shifts staying up on watch. They all crowded into the dorm room to get past the crowds of men and women in the hallway. Lund pulled out his hand laser and sat down on one of the chairs and faced the doorway.

"How well do you know some of the other cadets?" Lund finally asked in an effort to break the silence.

"I know the cadets on my floor really well," Gorski answered. "If something happens, we can count on the majority of them to lend us a hand.

"Good. How would you feel about spending the night elsewhere?" Lund looked at them to judge their reaction.

"We could do that, but how do we catch anyone playing cat and mouse?" Gorski was wondering. "If we are in another room, a professional team will go room to room while we are in Lock Down and hurt all of our friends looking for us. I prefer a straight up fight."

"Oh, we will give them a fight. That is, if they make the mistake of attacking tonight," Lund assured Gorski. "We have already planted surveillance cameras all over both of your rooms. We will be watching your rooms from mine. You want to give them a fight? That is exactly what they will get. When they enter your room, we will observe them on this," Lund held up a three inch by three inch screen pad. "Once they are in the room, we move to secure the hallway. When they come out, realizing you are not here, we hit them. All right?"

"Sounds like a good strategy," Gorski agreed. "You do realize that the dormitories will be full of cadets due to the sand storm Lock Down?"

"Yes we calculated that variable in our planning. Now, hurry up and pack your essentials, tooth brush, soap, and underwear. We may be staying together for a day or two," Lund instructed.

"Do we get any weapons?" Jack Harcourt inquired.

Lund motioned to Hodges, "Give them laser pistols." Lund knew he was violating Colonel Gorski's orders to not provide weapons to the cadets. But the sand storm had Lund concerned. It reminded him of Darktober when General Clark and her staff were ambushed and killed. He knew this was the perfect opportunity to kill someone. Over the loud winds, no one would hear a scream. If they were coming it will be tonight, Lund told himself.

Elektra Papanikolaou had already met her shadow. The woman knocked on her door and introduced herself as Private First Class Sara Stewart. She was a short girl of just over five feet tall with freckles on her face and a petite frame. Papanikolaou was concerned that her body guard was so tiny. As they spent some time speaking, the cadet learned that her body guard was fluent in Greek. Papanikolaou also learned that Stewart was twenty years old and had been born in London on old Earth and was raised in an orphanage due to her birth mother not having enough income to justify having children. She enlisted in the service at the age of seventeen and did well enough on her basic training and testing that she qualified for Military Intelligence Branch. Stewart was immediately ordered to join the MI platoon under Sergeant First Class Mark Lund on planet New Edinburgh. It had been Stewart's first and only assignment. Stewart, although petite and short, was well trained in hand to hand combat and she was a good shot with a laser pistol. She revealed that she had a black belt in karate. On her personal life, Papanikolaou learned that Stewart was single and had no romantic prospects at the moment.

"So none of the men in your unit show any interest in you?" Papanikolaou asked her.

Stewart shook her head side to side, "No. My platoon consists of seven men and forty-one women. The odds are not favorable for any of us girls to land one of the guys. Besides, I was raised in an orphanage and most men find that distasteful."

Elektra smiled at her, "So keep that to yourself until after a few dates. No sense blowing a potentially good thing before it even starts."

"The problem is that I never even get that first date," Stewart told her. "You do not understand the reality of my life, Elektra. I was abandoned as a child and never adopted. Most available men frown on that. I have never been able to observe from first hand interaction what a healthy relationship is all about. All I ever saw was kids living in despair with headmasters and guards that treated us all like trash. But enough about me. How about you, Elektra? Do you have any lovers in your life?"

"Yes, there is one. He is handsome, funny and very smart. But he loves studying about rocks. Rocks. Can you believe that? I really like him but I cannot get over the fact that he wants to spend his life digging through rocks."

"Nothing is perfect. Listen, if they are going to do anything it will be tonight," Stewart informed her. "I am not trying to scare you. I need you to be alert."

Elektra nodded slowly, "I would do the same if I were them. What is our plan?"

"We are waiting on Staszko and her shadow, LaShondra. We will be staying in another room for the evening. The attackers will enter your dormitory room and our surveillance cameras will get us pictures of the attackers. Those pictures will be downloaded immediately to my room and to the main computer at the Military Intelligence wing of the United Nations Building. If that computer locates a photographic match, we will know who they are. Get yourself a nice, comfortable, dark pair of clothes and your toothbrush. You will be stuck by my side for a while. Questions?"

"Do we tell my friends?"

"No. The less that the others know the better for them. Move out, cadet."

Elektra grabbed her gymnasium bag and began packing the items she had been instructed to bring. She liked her protector. She was blunt.

Jen Staszko and LaShondra Lewis were waiting for them in the new dormitory room. Staszko and Papanikolaou hugged.

"They say that this is the night they might come after us?" Elektra shuddered as she heard the winds howling outside of the dormitory.

"Yes, but we have the upper hand this time. We are expecting them." Staszko felt her pockets to make certain that she had her stun darts that Giles Lancer had sold them. She was prepared to get some revenge for the innocent families on the destroyed Transport and for Drayton Love-Easter.

Jurgen Doernitz bought a red rose from a floral store near the Academy and then ran to the women's dormitory as the warning alarms were sounding. Doernitz had been unable to get Melissa Harcourt out of his mind. In class he could not stop daydreaming about her. He ran up the stairs as fast as his legs would carry him and made it to Melissa's room quickly. He knocked on her door.

Melissa opened the door. He smiled at her and handed her the red rose. "I thought about you all day long."

She sighed, "Look, Jurgen, I appreciate the gesture. But you really need to go home."

Doernitz was confused by her words and the look on her face indicated that she was not happy to see him. "I don't understand. I thought...."

She took the rose from him and showed a flash of anger in her eyes. "Thought? Thought what? That we would be a couple like your sister and Porfirio? No, Jurgen. No. That is not me. You are a great guy, but I want to be a fighter pilot and see the universe. No man, not even you, will keep me from my dreams. You need to go home before the Lock Down is completed."

"I am not trying to steal you away from your dreams," Doernitz protested as he was now even more confused by the demeanor of the woman. "I want the same things that you do, to be a pilot. I just thought we could be really good for each other."

Melissa looked down at the ground, trying to find the right words to get rid of Doernitz so that she could move on to her next conquest. "Jurgen, I have many lovers and I need you to leave before the man I invited to stay the night gets here. When I need you to spend the night again, I will let you know. Go home."

She stepped back into her room and slammed the door in his face.

She leaned against her door and smelled the rose. Melissa realized that was a first, no one had ever brought her a flower before.

Doernitz on the other side of the door was speechless. He turned and saw several other female cadets staring at him. They had heard the whole conversation. Doernitz gave them a weak smile and slowly walked away, embarrassed by all of the stares from the other women in the dormitory hallway. He could hear the warnings from the computer broadcast that the Lock Down was going to be completed in fifteen minutes. Realizing he had best get to the home of his sister, Doernitz began to run as fast as he could. He estimated he should be able to make it home in time.

Ann Harcourt, Melissa's roommate, witnessed the cold treatment of Doernitz. Ann was glaring Melissa.

"He gives you a flower and you cut out his heart?" Ann sat up from her bed. "Really, Melissa. You ought to have your head examined. I could feel his vibes and he has a good spirit and noble intentions. Good men like that do not grow on trees."

Melissa sniffed the pretty flower, "You might be right, Ann. I think I made a bad decision here. But we are the only two female cadets that are Children of Athena. We are not like the others, Ann. We are special. We have gifts and abilities that make us better than the others. You know how it is, Ann. All of the normal human men just want to be with us so they can brag that they slept with one of us. I keep thinking all men are the same."

"Well they are not all the same." Ann went to the restroom to brush her teeth. Even though Melissa was her roommate, Ann found that she sometimes despised her. Melissa gave all of the Children of Athena a bad name with her behavior. Ann finished rinsing her mouth and turned toward Melissa. "If I were him, I would not be back. Not after that."

"What should I do?" Melissa whispered to herself, but Ann heard her.

"If it were me, I would go after him. But with the storm coming, you had better just stay here and hope he will talk to you tomorrow." Ann began rinsing her mouth with anti-bacterial mouth wash.

Melissa walked over to her bed and looked out the window. She could see the sand, and other debris flying around. With the backdrop of the red-orange New Edinburgh sky, it looked like death was coming. I hope you get home safely, she thought to herself.

Penelope Rosenburg had been both surprised and glad to receive the message from Les Gillis. She properly responded to him and made clear she wanted to see him again. She was relaxing in her office and monitoring twelve different items on her three dimensional broadcast screen on her far wall. One of the news items was the speech by the Glorious Leader, Vladimir Sikorsky, regarding the recent deaths of four separatist politicians on planet Cootron. She loved to hear his speeches, especially the ones in which he demanded that all people maintain their loyalty to each other. He was a classic politician; his words were both inspiring and confident. And the fact that he was Penelope's great-great grandfather gave her some pride. Sikorsky was denying any involvement in the tragic accidents on Cootron. He promised the citizens of Earth and Cootron that there would be an investigation into the deaths.

Another story was involving new advancements in the use of space craft to collect liquid iron from brown dwarfs as perfected by the Allen Corporation scientists. A third report was regarding the Dust Storm on New Edinburgh that was turning toward Clovis City. The reporter was live at the main hospital telling the audience that the city manager had ordered a Lock Down of the entire city. Due to the Enhancement Drugs her mother ingested throughout the gestation period, Penelope was able to use parts of her brain that increased her intellect and the ability to multi-task and watch all of these reports at the same time and grasp each story was as simple to her as another person adding two plus two.

It had been an uneventful day at work and Penelope was drinking a glass of Merlot wine to end the day. Ella Ragnarsson frantically pressed the red buzzer at her door and Penelope heard the chime inside her office and looked up at one of her security monitor screens on the wall to see that Ella was waiting outside.

"Come in," Penelope instructed her security chief.

Ella stormed in and pointed to the many three dimensional screens that Penelope had been watching. "Turn off those broadcasts. I have some news."

"Computer, cease broadcasts," Penelope said in response to Ella's demands. The three dimensional displays all disappeared. "I was really interested in some of those news reports. I hope your news is good."

"Better than good, more like urgent. My brother, Ivar, contacted me today from Clovis City. He said that the five cadet witnesses are still alive!" Ella approached the opened bottle of Merlot and poured herself a glass. "That means my sister Emma failed. Your father will be really pissed off when he finds out those five got away."

"Don't worry about my father," Penelope told her, trying to act as if she were stunned by the news. "Worry about his favorite wife, Magdalena. She is the vengeful one. My father only worries about keeping business strong and his people loyal. Beyond that, he really does not care. Magdalena is a barracuda. So the cadets are alive. Big deal. Let it go. Who will listen to them anyway? The whole situation is contained now. No one will listen to them." Penelope realized that she was subconsciously protecting Les Gillis. She reminded herself to be careful.

"No big deal?" Ella was clearly emotional over the subject. She was waiving her wine glass around as if to accentuate her point. "I am a Ragnarsson! My family is the best group of assassins in the eight solar systems! We never fail to complete a contract. My sister Emma just brought shame to our family. Our reputation will be tarnished by this. My father was furious when I told him."

Penelope knew Ella well enough that there was much more to this story coming. She drank from her wine glass and chose her words carefully. "What did your father decide to do?"

"We have a hit team in Clovis City right now!" Ella informed her. "Most of them worked with me during the Dark October hit. During the

Dust Storm, those five cadets are going to be taken, one by one."

"Taken?" Penelope put her elbows on her desk and rested her head on the palms of her hands. "And then what will happen to them?"

"Then they will all be fed to the creatures in the arena," Ella announced proudly. "The slaves and the workers on the Rosenburg Ranch will get a good show out of it. Although, I hear that one of your brothers has pictures of the gypsy girl and really likes her. So, she might be allowed to live if she plays her cards right."

Penelope was quiet for a few seconds, thinking about the danger Gillis and his friends were in. "How many were sent in to capture them?"

"Several," Ella told her after she took a drink of wine. "My older brother, Junior, is leading the team. Emma is with him so she can make amends for her screw up."

"How do they propose to get five cadets away from the Academy with all of the security, the marines, and the military intelligence, all of the people around and during a major dust storm?" Penelope wanted an answer to that. Her brilliant mind was calculating various scenarios on how a team could accomplish the goal. It would be easier just to kill the targets. Hit and run. But to kidnap? There had to be many alternative points of escape. She was surprised that the infamous Junior Ragnarsson would agree to such an impossible task.

"My brother has a plan. He always does. He will contact me when the job is done."

"Keep me in the loop," Penelope told her calmly. "I want to know everything."

"You will be the first to know," Ella assured her as she left the office.

Penelope drank some more of her wine. She pondered whether or not to contact Les Gillis and warn him of the contract out on him. She was certain that if she did send out a warning to the cadet her family would find out. And once she was discovered as a traitor to her family, she would be killed as her brother Cush had been. Or she would suffer a more painful death than Cush had, if that were possible.

The cadets at the Academy were rushing to their dormitories for cover. Most of them had never been exposed to a New Edinburgh Dust Storm before so they had little knowledge as to just how fierce the storm might become. Only the cadets that had lived on New Edinburgh for a several years before entering the Academy remembered the last one. The alarms were loud enough to get the message out to the population of Clovis City that this was not a drill. This was a serious weather warning, and loss of life could occur if ignored.

Marco Andolini and Mary Lincoln had gone to the Campus Cafeteria and eaten their brunch. They had joined Dirk Fenster, Klaus Rhinehard and April Mejia at the long table they had selected. Soon after, Marco's brother, Dominic Andolini joined them along with Harumi Shigeta.

They were cognizant of the eerie sound of the winds and the ominous alarms that seemed to perpetually wail.

"We should probably get back to our dorms," Lincoln stated the obvious. She leaned into Marco, looking into his eyes. "The question is your place or mine?"

Marco did not care that the others were watching them with interest. Until now, no one else knew that there was any attraction between the two, so their coupling was quite a surprise to all assembled. The cat was clearly out of the bag.

"Why don't we go to my place and after a couple of games of pool in the dormitory recreation center we can adjourn to my room?" Marco suggested. He recalled that Lincoln enjoyed playing pool and she was quite good at it.

Lincoln smiled as she was pleased he remembered how much she enjoyed the competition of pool. "That sounds like fun, fly boy." They gave each other a long, lingering kiss. The others looked away to give the couple some privacy.

Dominic was happy for his twin brother. When it came to the fairer sex, Marco normally was averse to relationships. He had many girlfriends in the past, but he never stayed involved with any of them for more than a week or two. Consequently, Marco had gained a reputation as a playboy. In reality, he was waiting for the one he really wanted, which was Mary Lincoln all along.

"We really should get going," Harumi warned them. They all noticed that the cafeteria staff was yelling for everyone to vacate the premises.

"Let's go," Dominic agreed.

The group rose to their feet and quickly followed the crowd of other cadets and campus staff to the exit.

As the wail of the winds grew more intense, Porfirio Cardenas was at his home in the married quarters of Clovis Academy. His two children were in their bedrooms, safe. His wife, Freya, was working the late shift at the hospital and would also be safe. The hospital had lock down walls that would slide down from the rooftop and connect to the cement ground. The storm would not harm the building. But his brother-in-law, Jurgen Doernitz, was not yet home. The alarms had been warning that the Lock Down was imminent. Cardenas paced the living area as the warning alarms continued. "Come on, kid," Cardenas whispered to himself. "Where are you? Lord please bring him home safe to us."

Cardenas pulled out his hand held holo-com device. "Computer, person to person, Jurgen Doernitz."

He waited for about fifteen seconds and heard the young man's voice. "Porfirio, I am running home right now!" Doernitz was breathing heavily. Cardenas could hear the howl of the strong winds over the device. Doernitz had been running as fast as he could since he was tossed aside by Melissa Harcourt. The winds and the sands had been pounding the cadet pilot mercilessly. Doernitz was covering his face with his hood from his cadet uniform, but he still suffered some minor cuts from the coarse sand.

"The alarms are reporting only a few minutes before Lock down!"

Cardenas told him. "How far away are you?"

"Not far!" Doernitz was yelling over the winds. "I'll make it!"

"Remember that the married quarters will be covered by a round metallic bubble," Cardenas described the safety measures of Clovis City. All housing areas had a metallic shield that would cover the entire subdivision and protect all of the homes. This would allow the neighbors to interact and leave their individual homes to visit one another while the crisis was occurring. All young Doernitz had to do was be in the perimeter of the subdivision before the Lock Down was initiated and he would be safe.

"I know! I am already in the subdivision!" Doernitz sounded like he was celebrating that fact. "I will be home soon!"

Cardenas smiled and praised God. Cardenas knew that the Lord was watching over Doernitz. Have faith, Cardenas told himself.

What the two young men did not realize at the time was that by leaving the dormitory building when he did, Doernitz quite possibly escaped a night of intrigue and terror.

CHAPTER EIGHT

Ivar Ragnarsson met his brother Junior, sister Emma and the rest of the team at the private landing strip a few kilometers west of the cadet dormitory buildings. The dark red colored Raumschiff was resting under a large Hangar area with dozens of other space craft. Civilian employees were securing all of the space craft to the concrete and metal landing area with steel cables that connected to the ground and on specialized hooks on each ship. Ivar hugged his siblings and informed them that he brought his personal glider to take them all to the dormitories. Ivar was having to yell as the howl of the winds were loud. They all walked quickly to the light blue glider with white trim that Ivar had waiting for them. Ivar's ship was similar to the one the hospital sent to pick up cadets Bragg and Gillis. It could hover and fly about thirty feet in the air and comfortably transport up to twenty people. Ivar's father had purchased the craft for him.

As they all stepped on board Ivar's ship they could hear the computer generated warning: "Fifteen minutes to Lock Down! Fifteen Minutes!"

Ivar sat in the driver's seat of his glider and then flew them at best speed to the dormitory buildings. He was excited that he was finally able to help out his family. As children, the Ragnarsson's were taught by their father how to kill. For Ivar, it began when his father forced him to kill his own pet. It had been a small dog, a Yorkie he had named Scout. Ivar had to strangle the pet to death while his father forced him to look into the eyes of the dog as life slipped away from it. Ivar did the deed to make his father proud of him. Afterward, Ivar cried over what he had done and would have nightmares about the look the dog gave him as he had killed him. He had loved that dog and he murdered him and the guilt over it never left Ivar. His father instructed the boy that killing ones pet makes you stronger. As he grew into his teenage years, Ivar was forced to kill slaves or prisoners using knives, lasers and other weapons. Ivar's father told him that these acts were all to be taken as training to learn how to kill and to prepare Ivar to be tougher emotionally. Ivar and each of the siblings that he grew up with, Junior, Emma, Ella, Eva, Ulla and Ellis, went through similar instruction and training with father.

The team of assassins could feel the powerful winds slamming against the hull of Ivar Ragnarsson's glider. Junior knew that their window of opportunity was rapidly closing. They needed to be inside the dormitories before the protective metal bulkheads slammed shut.

Most of the population of Clovis City had been astute enough to find shelter when the first warnings were issued. Several procrastinators were running on the paved streets covering their faces to protect their eyes from the coarse sand.

Junior looked over his team and concluded that they were prepared to proceed. During the flight from Rosenburg's Ranch to Clovis City they had memorized the faces of the five targets and their friends at the Academy. They had committed the room numbers that the five cadets lived in to memory. They would enter the rooms by stealth, stun the cadets, bind them and wait for the Lock Down to end. Then they would then take the cadets to the flight pad, load them aboard their Raumschiff and transport them back to Rosenburg's Ranch where all of the men would be fed to the pets in captivity. The two women would become wives for breeding purposes for some of the Rosenburg men. The plan was simple. Any cadet interlopers were to be stunned only. To the chagrin of Montrose, no collateral damage was allowed on this mission. Junior paired his sister Emma with his wife Dulce. The fact that Emma made such a grievous error in failing to kill the cadets before would be addressed by their father at a later date. This mission was the only way for Emma to demonstrate that she was competent and therefore avoid father's wrath.

Junior felt the ship landing. Ivar was yelling that they were near the Dormitory buildings. Junior followed Dulce and Emma off of the Glider. Nikko was behind him, followed by Montrose, Quintana, Chang and Prescott. They covered their faces due to the harsh winds. Ivar secured his Glider to metal docking cables which would hold the ship in place during the sand storm.

"This way!" Ivar screamed above the howling winds.

The team followed the young cadet to the men's dormitory. Junior looked at the tall building. It was twenty-two floors in height and had a massive basement area where the laundromat and storage rooms were. He knew that it housed thousands of young men studying to be pilots, soldiers, weapons experts, scientists, engineers and other various trades. The women's dormitory was the same but slightly larger as there were more women cadets than men. Ivar placed his palm on the identity scanner on the front door and the doors slid open for him. Junior entered the lobby first, followed by his men. Ivar did not join them as his instructions were to join the women on their mission. He went with Dulce and Emma to take them to the women's dormitory.

In the lobby of the men's dormitory, Nikko was standing next to Junior. They quickly scanned the scene, as they had been trained to do, and saw there were dozens of male and female students rushing back and forth. To the right of the entrance was a huge recreation room with pool tables, chess boards, poker dealer tables and machines for the newest three dimensional computer games. Many students were testing their skill against others at the various tables. Others were watching, some occasional cheers would be heard from one or more of the spectators. Junior saw a few couples kissing and getting ready to rush up the stairs to spend the night together. Typical University atmosphere, he thought to himself.

"Over there," Nikko pointed toward a pool table in the corner.

They observed several of Gorski's friends playing a game of pool. "I don't see any of our targets with them."

Junior remembered the students from the photographs they studied on the flight over. The twins, Marco and Dominic Andolini were there, arms around their girlfriends, Mary Lincoln and Harumi Shigeta. Klaus Rhinehard and April Mejia were also with them. The cadets were laughing and teasing Mary for having knocked in the white ball by accident.

"Good. Hopefully those six will stay here and be out of the way," Junior whispered to Nikko. "Looks like they plan on staying here for a while."

Nikko nodded and made his way to the south stair case with Prescott. They had been assigned the task of capturing Les Gillis and his room was located on the southernmost portion of his hallway.

Junior and Montrose paired off and walked calmly toward the escalator. They were going to go after their assignment: Yuri Gorski.

Chang and Quintana were assigned to kidnap Michel Evart. They took the stairs, walking slowly past the numerous cadets that were running up and down the metal steps in an attempt to draw little to no attention to themselves.

Junior made a mental note that the hallways in the dormitory were wide enough for four men to comfortably walk side by side. All of the entrances to the individual dormitory rooms were sliding doors and were not flush to the hallway, they were about two feet indented between the hall and doorway. Junior knew that two feet would provide cover for them in a laser fight, or it would be protection for the enemy.

They could hear the warnings: "Lock Down in five minutes!"

Nikko and Prescott made it to the fourth floor, where Lester Gillis' room was. The two hired killers walked down the hallway, passing students that were talking about the coming storm and other issues. Ivar Ragnarsson had given the men Gillis' room number. They nonchalantly approached his door. The most important aspect of a successful mission was to avoid attracting unwanted attention. Nikko kept watch as Prescott picked the lock on the door, using a small hand held computerized device that sent a digital command to the security system to override the set codes. It worked and the door slid open.

Nikko followed Prescott into the room and they allowed the door to slide shut behind them. Both men had drawn their hand lasers and were ready to fire. As they scanned the room, they both heard the meow from one of the beds. They saw the black and white cat, staring at them inquisitively.

"Just a damn cat!" Nikko spat as Prescott searched the bathroom and shower area. Nikko looked under the beds. The two men opened the two walk in closets finding them full of cadet uniforms and other civilian clothing.

No sign of Lester Gillis.

"Where the hell is he?" Nikko looked to Prescott.

"Anything I say would be purely speculation," Prescott said with his English accent. "Perhaps with Gorski and Evart or his old girlfriend

Sophia DuBravac?"

Nikko sat on the bed and the cat began purring and rubbing against him. Nikko snarled and slapped the cat hard. Cosmos screeched and ran for cover, limping under the bed. Nikko pulled out his holo-com device from his pants pocket. "Computer, are you still hacked into the Clovis Academy system?"

"Yes," his palm computer answered.

"Give me the time that Lester Brey Gillis entered the men's dormitory," Nikko instructed.

"Lester Gillis entered the building at six a.m. this morning," the computer answered.

"And no information as to whether or not he left?"

"The Dormitory does not keep that information," the computer replied. "However, he did check into the Cordell Hull United Nations Hospital approximately forty-five minutes ago and was admitted for x-rays."

"How far is the hospital?" Prescott demanded.

"Two kilometers," the computer replied.

"We'll never make it!" Nikko told him. "The hospital will be locked down by the time we run over there."

"Each emergency facility keeps an emergency entrance," the computer told them. "I can open the entrance for you, once you have arrived."

"So we can get into the hospital even if it is locked down?" Nikko wanted to clarify.

"Yes."

"Let's move!" Prescott told Nikko.

The two men ran out of the room and down the hallway. They needed to be out of the men's dormitory before the metal defenses sealed them inside. But then they needed to survive the coming sand storm when they were outside and exposed. Running two kilometers was not much of a task for two men in decent physical conditioning. But to run in this weather would tax the constitution of the best and the strongest.

Nikko made it to the exit of the dormitory as the metal barricade began lowering from the rooftop. Prescott was two steps behind him. Both men heard the sound of the metal lowering and were greeted rudely by the fierce winds. They began to run, covering their faces with their black leather jackets. Soon the heart of the storm would be crossing through Clovis City. Prescott knew they had better be inside before then, or they would most certainly be dead.

Chang and Quintana moved into Evart and Harcourt's room just as Nikko and Prescott had done when they infiltrated Les Gillis' room. Chang and Quintana searched the room and found nothing. Evart and Harcourt were not there.

Quintana and Chang sat on one of the two beds. Quintana scratched his head and looked around the room with the eyes of a carnivore searching for prey. Quintana squinted his eyes and concentrated on a small object across from him.

"Where are they?" Chang asked looking around the room. He watched as Quintana stood up and slowly walked over to the far right corner of the room. "What is it?"

Quintana shushed Chang as he reached up with his right hand. He found a small lens device that was only a quarter of an inch in diameter imbedded in the wall. Quintana crushed the device with his fingers. It was a small Brackenridge Corporation surveillance camera. Quintana knew only one organization that used that form of device for spying and that was the United Nations Military Intelligence. The militzia as some civilians referred to them. They were the elite of the entire Space Command.

"They were waiting for us," Quintana said in a whisper as he swallowed hard. These cadets were not the average target, Quintana thought to himself. They had connections that wielded the power to arrest and the force of law. He had no desire to spend the rest of his life on the prison planet Cootron. Quintana determined that the time had come to abort the mission and withdraw. "We had better make ourselves scarce. I have a feeling this is a set up."

Down the hallway, Lund, Gorski, Evart, Harrison, Jack Harcourt and Hodges watched on the small broadcast screens as Chang and Quintana entered Evart's dormitory room.

"Okay, we have contact!" Lund smiled with excitement. "I hope our master computer can get us a match on these two. I bet there will be another team in your room." Lund motioned to Gorski and Harrison.

Hodges was typing furiously on his holographic keyboard as he sent the video feed and still photographs of the two men to the master computer back at the Military Intelligence headquarters.

"Are we just going to sit here?" Harcourt asked impatiently. These men were sent to harm his friends and the Child of Athena wanted to arrest them immediately.

"Wait," Lund held up his hand to Harcourt. "Be patient. Let the others reveal themselves."

"What about Les?" Evart asked suddenly. "Didn't you get any surveillance in his room?"

"No, regrettably there was not enough time," Lund responded. "Your other friend is still at the hospital. I have one of my best men on him. He will be fine."

"They're here," Hodges spoke up, pointing to the computer screen. All of them watched as Junior Ragnarsson and Montrose entered Gorski and Harrison's room.

"Let's move. We get the two men in Evart's room first," Lund ordered.

Hodges ordered the computer to slowly open the door to Lund's room. There were cadets kissing against the walls, others were engaged in conversation. Lund and Hodges saw that Quintana and Chang were running up the hallway toward them, with hand lasers in their right hands held close to their right side. They were clearly scared as Lund could see the whites in both of their eyes. Lund and Hodges stepped out into the hall with their hand lasers aimed at the two men.

"Stop right there. Drop your weapons!" Lund ordered them.

The average man or woman would have been startled by the sight of Lund and Hodges aiming weapons in their direction. Quintana and Chang were not the average type of men. Both Quintana and Chang had trained for many years so that they would be able to react to any imminent threat that crossed their paths. Instead of dropping their weapons as Lund had demanded, Quintana dived to the floor, while Chang slid onto the floor on the opposite side of him. Both men were instinctively aiming their lasers in the direction of Lund and Hodges.

Equal to the task, Lund and Hodges were not the average men either. Both had gone through three months of military basic training, several more months of Military Intelligence training and had been put through an hour of martial arts instruction each day for their entire military careers. Lund was certainly no shrinking violet. Hodges had ice in his veins and never felt fear or stress in any given situation. So when the two assassins refused Lund's polite offer of surrender, they fired their hand lasers. Quintana was hit in the chest by laser streams from both Lund and Hodges. Quintana went limp as he fell unconscious.

Chang yelled loud enough for Junior and Montrose to hear him in the other room as he fired back in the direction of the tallest adversary, his size making him the easiest to shoot at effectively. Hodges was hit and he fell backwards into the dormitory room. Evart caught the man before he hit the ground. After Evart was able to pull Hodges inside the room,

Harrison and Gorski charged out into the hallway to see Lund firing at Chang again, the blast narrowly missing the Asian assassin.

The random cadets that had been in the hallway had scattered when the laser fire began. In Gorski and Harrison's room, Junior and Montrose heard their comrade's warning. The two removed the computer controls to the sliding doors and slowly opened them manually. They spied out into the hallway to see the laser fight ensuing. By now, Harcourt and Evart were also in the hallway. It was five against Chang.

"Not very sporting of them," Junior whispered as he aimed his laser pistol at the target that would give them the most trouble in combat. Any and all assassins under Junior were taught to neutralize any Children of Athena first. In any combat situation it would be a mistake to allow one of them to use their genetically altered powers of mind control. With that in mind, Junior fired at the back of the cotton white skinned cadet named Jack Harcourt first.   Jack Harcourt felt as if he was being electrocuted as he was hit by a laser blast. He went spinning to the ground without emitting a scream. Evart saw his friend crumple to the floor. He had the laser pistol that had been in Hodges' belt and had made sure it was set for enough power to stun a man. Evart leaned out the doorway and fired at the men that had shot Harcourt. Evart cursed at himself as his shot missed wide to the left of his target. Junior and Montrose returned fire, forcing Evart to duck back behind the doorway. Gorski and Harrison rolled behind the door frames across the hallway from their location and began firing their laser pistols at their opponents.

Lund fired again and hit Chang in his mid-section. Chang did not cry out as he simply dropped his laser and his head hit the floor with a thud. Lund was not able to celebrate the fact that he had knocked Chang out of the fire fight as he was hit in the back by a blast fired by Montrose. Lund slumped forward to the floor.

"We need to withdraw," Junior told Montrose the obvious. Three against two was not good odds, even if one of the opponents was not a good shooter. The two assassins began running backwards toward the south of the building where another stair case was located. As the two assassins were running, Gorski and Harrison gave chase while Evart stayed back and tied bindings to Chang's arms and legs. He then bound Quintana.

Naturally, the yells by Chang and the sounds of the laser fire brought much attention in the dormitory hallway. Several cadets began opening their doors to see what all of the yelling and excitement was about. As they were running down the hallway, Junior and Montrose were stunning several cadets, firing on a few of them at point blank range. One of the cadets that had opened his door due to the commotion was Arch Frazier. He regretted that he had been so curious as he caught a laser blast in the abdomen. He fell backwards onto the floor.

Gorski and Harrison were firing their laser pistols and were aggressively advancing on Montrose and Junior, just as they were trained in their classes. They would run to each doorway and take cover behind the extension of the walls around the doors. They would fire a volley of several laser bursts at the two would be assassins and then advance to the next doorway extension.

"These kids are fucking good!" Montrose hissed to Junior.

Junior nodded his agreement and was wishing he had brought more men. He hoped that one of Gorski's friends, Dominic Andolini, stayed out of the fight. Junior was impressed by Dominic's marksmanship scores that demonstrated he did not miss.

Due to the potential of intervention by Dominic Andolini and others, Junior had a strong desire to end the cat and mouse game and withdraw. He and Montrose kept returning fire at the two cadets as the backed up down the hallway toward the stairwell exits.

Gorski and Harrison were both breathing heavily due to the heightened adrenaline. They were pushing the two unknown men back by continuing to fire their laser pistols and aggressively advancing toward them. "If they get to the stairs..." Gorski warned as a laser blast flew by his head.

"We need to make sure they do not make it!" Harrison affirmed he was on the same page as Gorski. At that point, Evart was able to catch up to his friends.

"The other two are bound tight!" Evart told them, dodging behind a wall slamming hard against the door as Montrose and Junior fired in their direction.

"Jack is stunned, so was Arch!" Evart informed Gorski and Harrison as he fired his hand laser in the direction of Junior and Montrose.

"They shot about ten other cadets as well."

Junior and Montrose were only a few feet from the door to the south stairwell. They hoped that they would be able to avoid capture and come back at a later date to free their two team members. The mission would have to be completed at another time and place. Montrose was ready to reach for the door. Junior pulled out a concussion grenade from his black leather jacket pocket and nodded to Montrose. It would give the pursuing cadets a headache and disorient them long enough to cover their escape. Junior pressed the button on the grenade and rolled it in Gorski's direction. Harrison saw the weapon rolling down the hall and bouncing a few times on the carpeted floor. He knew it was an explosive device, but was unsure what kind.

"Grenade!" Harrison yelled.

Gorski and Harrison ran backwards and Evart dodged behind one of the doorway walls. The explosion shook the floor and created enough grey smoke to obscure the entire hallway. The cadets below on level four felt the shaking of the floor due to the blast. They wrote it off as part of the Dust Storm. Gorski had covered his ears just before the blast. In their training, Gorski, Harrison and Evart had been instructed to guard their hearing if an opponent used any kind of explosive device. Gorski rolled on the ground and turned his head toward the stair exit. He looked down the hall and could barely see anything due to the thick grey smoke. Gorski squinted his eyes and thought he saw the stairwell door open.

Junior and Montrose did not expect to run into the other members of the Gorski Gang after gaining access to the stairwell. They were wrong. Marco Andolini and Mary Lincoln were stepping into the fifth floor ledge of the stairwell which led to the doorway to the hallway. They had finished playing several games of pool, shuffle board and some of the computer games in the recreation center. All of the Gorski Gang members that were playing decided to meet at the Andolini's room for drinks. Since the elevator lifts might shut down during the Lock Down, the cadets deduced that it would be safer to take the stairs up to the fifth floor. None of them had a clue what was waiting for them on the other side of the stairwell door.

Junior and Montrose noticed Marco Andolini and Mary Lincoln as soon as they opened the stairwell doors. The two assassins rushed the two cadets and fired their lasers at them. Marco let out a cry to his friends as he was hit in the chest by a laser blast. He fell to the metal floor with a loud clanging noise. Lincoln was also hit and fell on top of Marco. Junior and Montrose rushed into the stairwell.

The others with Marco and Lincoln watched them both crumple to the metal stairwell after being stunned by the laser blasts. Klaus Rhinehard was the closest to the stairwell door and slid against the wall and waited for the attackers to enter.

Montrose ran in first and was hit in the face by Klaus. He staggered backwards, against the stairwell safety rails, almost flipping over them. Klaus growled and rushed at Montrose, unwilling to give the unknown attacker any chance to recover from his punch. Junior was in the stairwell and saw that his partner was in peril. He also noticed that Dirk Fenster, April Mejia, Harumi Shigeta and Dominic Andolini were running up the stairs, glaring at him.

Junior cursed at the sight of Dominic. He was the one cadet he did not want to take on in a weapons fight. Junior began firing his laser pistol at the crowd of Gorski Gang members, hoping to hit the marksman Andolini first. Since they were in a cluster, Junior had to try hard to miss. Mejia and Fenster were hit and fell onto the stairs. Shigeta, with her fists up, almost made it to Junior, but he stunned her and she fell at his feet.

Dominic was able to reach Junior and knocked his laser pistol out of his hand. He hit Junior in the stomach, causing the hired killer to double over. Junior pulled out of his pocket a stun dart and desperately stabbed it into Dominic's shoulder. The Italian stiffened and fell down onto the metal stairs.

Montrose and Klaus had gotten several good punches in on each other. Montrose, who was far more experienced in fighting, used Klaus's forward motion and flipped the young cadet over the metal safety rails. The cadet screamed as he fell to the level below him. He tried to break his fall by holding his arms out in front. The impact on the metal stairs caused his right wrist to snap and his left arm to break at just above the elbow. His head and body bounced on the stairs and he rolled over on his side as he cried out in pain.

Junior recovered his dropped laser pistol as his eyes darted in every direction to see if any further trouble was coming in their direction.

This was getting out of hand, he told himself. Montrose's nose was bleeding as was his lower lip, indicating that the Rhinehard kid put a good beating on the man. Junior motioned for Montrose to follow him upstairs. If Rhinehard could inflict so much damage on an experienced killer as Montrose, Junior began to worry that the better trained cadets like Gorski or Harrison could prove to be far better adversaries. Montrose was by Junior's side as the ascended the stairs. They ran quickly.

As they made it up to the sixth floor, they heard the fifth floor door fly open. Junior was certain that it was Gorski, Evart and Harrison. He and Montrose continued to ascend the stairs, making their way to the rooftop.

Brandon Harcourt heard the laser fire and the screams while in his dormitory room. He had invited Bao Mingjuan over so that the two could spend the night together. Brandon was one of the five Children of Athena that attended the Academy. Bao came from a modest family with a few dozen siblings from Lynott's Land and was studying computer sciences. She was often mistaken for her twin sister, Li, who was a botany student. Things had been getting interesting between Bao and Brandon when their kissing turned into heavy petting and soon expanded into the removal of clothing. But when the two cadets were interrupted by the noise in the hallway, they both began to quickly throw their clothing back on so that they could go out of the room and see what was happening.

Gorski and Harrison checked on Marco and Lincoln. They were relieved to find that their friends were only stunned. They carefully entered the stairwell as Evart joined them. They found Dominic and

Harumi Shigeta on the level five portion of the stairwell. On the stairs leading up to the fifth floor were Fenster and Mejia, both not moving. They could hear Klaus on the fourth floor stairs, moaning in agony.

Gorski checked Shigeta's pulse and were relieved to find that she was only stunned. Harrison gave Gorski a thumbs up regarding Dominic's status. Both were going to be okay. Evart entered the staircase, a laser pistol in his right hand. Another cadet, Brandon Harcourt, was with him. Bao Mingjuan was right behind them, buttoning her blouse up.

"What the..." Brandon Harcourt began when he saw the other four cadets lying in the stairwell. Gorski covered his mouth with his left hand.

"Shhhh!" Gorski said softly. "Can you get some others to help Klaus downstairs? He's hurt bad."

Brandon Harcourt nodded.

"We will be advancing upstairs," Gorski told him. "Once we get up there, get to Klaus."

"Yes," Brandon Harcourt nodded again; his eyes were wide with disbelief. A real laser battle was happening in the middle of the Men's Dormitory. The recruiters for the Academy forgot to mention that could be a possibility.

He watched as Gorski fired several shots upstairs and began running up to the sixth floor with Harrison right behind him, firing his laser as well. Evart was close behind, firing. Brandon Harcourt saw some laser fire returned from above. He waited a few seconds and ran back to the fifth floor and banged on the nearest door. A cadet pilot named Dino

Black opened the door. The look in his eyes indicated that he had heard the commotion in the hallway. He was wearing a pair of underwear and was pulling a button up dress shirt on as he faced Brandon. Standing behind Black was a half-naked woman that Brandon recognized as engineering student Fara Kiesbye. The dormitories were a great place to meet for sex and Brandon was glad to see that he and Bao were not the only two that had been interrupted.

"Brandon? What the hell is going on?" Black demanded.

"I need your help. Klaus is hurt really badly," Brandon Harcourt said with urgency. Dino Black, who was a cadet pilot and familiar with the Rhinehard brothers, nodded and followed Harcourt without question. They joined Mingjuan and the three rushed down the stairs to the injured cadet. Mingjuan looked over his arms and grimaced at the sight of his broken arm.

While the other cadets were lending a hand to the injured, Gorski was making his way to the seventh floor, firing an occasional laser to keep the opponents above honest. Soon, he made it to the last level of the stairwell and the roof emergency exit door was to Gorski's left. The two men were gone. Gorski deduced that the only place the two attackers could be was on the roof of the building. If Gorski, Evart and Harrison walked out that door, they would most certainly be ambushed. Evart and Harrison joined Gorski on the last floor of the stairwell and looked at him for direction.

"They are on the roof," Gorski said with certainty.

"If we go out there, they will cut us down!" Harrison stated the obvious.

"Unless we have some help," Evart stated calmly. "I can go back and wake up Jack, Lund and Hodges. I have smelling salts. We have the six of us rush them. They can't shoot us all. What do you say?"

Gorski nodded, "Okay. But hurry! I don't want them getting out on another stairways. Maybe some of the cadets that were not stunned can get up here and help."

The three men knew that the emergency exits to the roof could not be opened from the outside unless you had been cleared by security. Evart ran down the stairs skipping many steps in his rush to bring reinforcements.

"Did you get a good look at their faces? Are these the ones that killed Dray?" Harrison asked Gorski.

"No. It is not the same guys. That was my first thought, but I have never seen these two before. Drew, if we go out on that roof, we will be exposed to the Sand Storm."

"I know that."

From down below, the cries of pain from Klaus reached Gorski and Harrison.

Gorski pulled out his holo-com device and spoke into it. "Michel, get the other cadets in the building to stand guard at all of the top level stair wells. If these last two try and get off the roof by blowing a door off, I want them to have some opposition. Call Rolf, he is somewhere in the building. He can help us. And hurry."

"I'm on it!" Evart responded.

Evart had used smelling salts on Lund, Hodges and Jack Harcourt. As the three men began waking up Evart ran to wake up the Andolini brothers, Lincoln, Mejia, Shigeta, Frazier and Fenster. To his chagrin, the smelling salts did not work on Dominic. He remained still as if sleeping under the influence of some powerful drug. Evart pulled out his holo-com device while waiting for everyone to wake up.

"Rolf, this is Michel. Can you hear me?" Evart spoke into his device.

Rolf Rhinehard was in the recreation room with about a four hundred other cadets, playing the computer three dimensional games. One of Amir al-Nasser's widows was giving Rolf a massage on his muscular shoulders. He heard his holo-com device alert him that Evart was calling. He pulled his holo-com from his belt and ordered the device to respond.

"Yes, Michel, I read you," Rolf answered.

"Rolf, round up all of the cadets there with you," Evart instructed him. "We need guards posted at the three emergency exits on to the rooftops on the north, east and south stairwells. This is life or death. The guys that killed Dray just attacked again. Get as many as you can."

"I'm on it!" Rolf turned his attention to the other cadets in the student break room. "Listen up! There was an attack! We need to block the emergency exits to the roof!"

"Who was attacked?" James Cobb asked.

"That doesn't matter! An attack on one of us is an attack on all of us," Cadet Pepito Calderon yelled out.

Rolf directed the cadets to go up to the roof emergency doors and stand guard. "If anyone other than a fellow cadet comes through the doors we need to restrain them."

Rolf ordered Calderon to lead a group to guard the north emergency exit and he selected cadet pilot Pierre Zerbe to lead a group to guard the east. Rolf turned to Bragg Gang member James Cobb, and as much as it pained Rolf to ask the man for help, and sent him to the south stairwell. Each of the three selected cadets rounded up about two dozen other cadets each to assist. Satisfied that the stairwell exits were covered, Rolf left this computer game and was walking toward the stairs with Anjuli al-Nasser following him.

Evart assisted Harumi Shigeta up and told her to breathe slowly and lean against the wall until she could focus. He next concentrated on helping April Mejia when he was contacted by Rolf. "Michel, I have all three stairwells patrolled. What next?"

"Find some cadets that are studying medicine," Evart instructed him. "Your brother was hurt. Klaus is in really bad shape. Get up to the fifth floor with help. Hurry."

The mention of his older brother being harmed caused Rolf to feel like someone reached into his chest and crushed his heart. He turned around and looked at the young faces of the remaining cadets in the recreation room, "Is there anyone here studying medicine?"

Two male cadets raised their hands.

"Follow me to the fifth floor. Someone needs immediate medical attention!" Rolf told them. The two cadets followed without question as he led them up the stairs to the fifth floor. The three were running as fast as their legs could carry them. "What are your names?"

"I'm Robert Windfohr, a pre-med candidate," the closest cadet said.

"Clark Blundell," the second told Rolf. "I am in my last year of pre-medical school, just like Robert."

The three men ran up to the fifth floor and heard Klaus Rhinehard's moans. He was on the floor, his legs moving about as if the act of moving them would somehow take the pain away. Mejia was kneeling next to him, hugging his left leg, and crying. Windfohr and Blundell both asked Mejia to move. They looked at Rhinehard's two arms and immediately recognized the fractures. Li Mingjuan, who had been with Blundell, saw her sister Bao and hugged her.

"Klaus, by Valhalla and Wotan," Rolf said softly when he looked upon his injured brother. The sight of the bone protruding through the elder Rhinehard's left arm was too much for Rolf to stomach. Rolf stood and faced the wall as he silently prayed to Tyr the God of War to watch over and protect his injured brother. The Rhinehard siblings had been raised to worship the Norse Gods by their mother. Due to the rise in extreme nationalism and genealogy awareness, many from old Earth began to embrace the old religions as a part of their once lost cultures. For many humans it was a way to find commonality with others that lived in the same geographical area.

"Someone bring us some hot water, blankets and we need wood, straight, so we can splint the broken bones." Blundell instructed, pointing at cadets to get the items he requested. "Does anyone have any pain killers?"

"Would straight liquor help?" Marco asked, looking down at Klaus with concern in his eyes.

"Yes, anything," Windfohr nodded. "We have to set his bones. He has some major breaks. We will need some strong men to hold him down. On the wall, at the end of the hallway, there should be some first aid kits. Bring them to us. There are supposed to be some pain killers in them."

"How did it happen?" Rolf asked.

"He fell down the stairs," Shigeta answered as she stroked Dominic's hair. She could not understand why her lover would not wake up.

Dino Black, Brandon Harcourt and Arch Frazier arrived with the items the medical students requested. Li and Bao Mingjuan offered to help the pre-med students.

"Please help him," Mejia said between sobs. "He's in so much pain." Shigeta was comforting her friend by holding her close to her side. It was obvious that Mejia really cared for the injured Rhinehard.

"Where is Evart?" Rolf asked.

Marco pointed up the stairwell.

All of the cadets that had been stunned were still not one hundred percent themselves. They were suffering from dehydration, dizziness and an inability to fully concentrate. After Evart had used smelling salts to wake up Lund and Hodges, the two soldiers had injected themselves with one booster of adrenaline and a second of concentrated liquid vapor to hydrate themselves. The other cadets watched Lund and Hodges use a third hyper dermic needle to inject themselves with vitamins A, B, B6, B12, C, D, E, K, niacin, folic acid, calcium, ginseng, beta carotene, iron and zinc. The third injection was to jump start their physical abilities following the effects of having been stunned by one of the laser blasts. The Space Command medical experts had determined that the human body, after suffering a stun blast, needed to recover from the dehydration side effect quickly before going back into action. So, every soldier and marine was issued a packet of the three injections.

Lund, seeing the look in the eyes of the numerous cadets surrounding the area, knew that they would be willing to help. He would not be able to rely on the cadets that had been hit by a stun laser. They would probably not be able to make it up the many flights of stairs due to the effects of the laser. Lund looked at Brandon Harcourt, Dino Black, Lila Zapata and several other cadets that had not been hit by weapon fire.

"I need you all," Lund pointed at them. "Get some heavy sweat shirts with hoods on quick. We are going out onto the rooftop. You need to have your bodies covered to protect you from the coarse sands."

Without questioning the orders, the cadets all ran to their rooms and quickly returned with the thick clothing Lund had directed them to retrieve. Marco and Lincoln also grabbed some thick hooded sweats with the Clovis Academy logo on the front and gave them to Lund.

"Some extras for you and Yuri, and the others!" Marco said, breathing hard. The stun blast he received had taken a lot of his energy. He glanced down on the floor at his brother, Dominic. The villains that attacked them had stabbed Dominic with one of those pen shaped darts. Lund had consoled Shigeta and Marco and implored them to not worry as Dominic would recover fully after about ten to twelve hours of a near comatose state.

"Thank you," Hodges told them, taking the thicker clothing.

"All, right, let's move it!" Lund began moving toward the stairwell.

"Wait!" Arch Frazier waived at them, trying to stand up. He felt like he was going to pass out. His body was craving water or some form of liquid energy drink. "Wait. The sand, the lighter colored sand. It has qualities similar to magnesium. It can be flammable at a high temperature. If you rush the roof, there will be tons of that sand swirling around due to the sand storm. If that stuff ignites, it could be a mini-firestorm."

"He's right!" Li Mingjuan confirmed.

"That gives me a really good idea, kid. Thanks," Lund told him. "Let's move out!"

Lund led the group of cadets to the roof emergency door where Gorski, Evart and Harrison were waiting for them.

Lund, Hodges, Brandon Harcourt, Black, Evart, Zapata, Harrison, Gorski and several other cadets were ready to rush the attackers. They all had put on thick sweat shirts with hoods and had thick gloves on their hands.

On the rooftop, Montrose and Junior had been busy. They had placed trip wires at each door to release stun and flame darts when activated. The two hired killers knew that the men's dormitory housed thousands of cadets. If Gorski and his friends were able to rally a large group of their fellow students, then escape would be nearly impossible. The only way to crush the morale of the cadets was to roast several of them alive. The flame darts, Junior believed, would accomplish that goal. The weapons would cause casualties, which was in direct violation of their orders. Given the way their mission was going, Junior was concerned that they may have to kill a thousand cadets to escape.

If Gorski or Evart fell victim to the weapons, then it was just as well. Junior was certain that this mission was officially a failure anyway. Junior had analyzed the events in his mind. He and his team had either been set up or the cadets were waiting for them, as if they knew that the hit team was going to attack. In any event, he had grossly underestimated the cunning of the cadets. He and Montrose were going to have to fight to free their partners Chang and Quintana. They would need to escape and return on another time and another place to complete the mission. But for now, chaos was the order of the day. Kill some of the enemy, which would test the resolve of the survivors, and then watch to see if the others flee in fear.

Lund and Hodges handed out hand lasers to the other cadets. Lund made sure that all of the students that had volunteered to venture out onto the rooftop were armed.

"When we open this door, the two men on the roof will start shooting at you," Lund told them. "I cannot guarantee your safety. This is strictly voluntary. Those two will be desperate. They are getting pounded by the sand and the winds. Hopefully they will not be in any shape to fight back."

"Enough talk," Harrison told Lund. "This ends here and now."

"Agreed," Lund said as he showed the group a grenade that he had in his right hand. "Crack open the door. I am going to throw out a thermite grenade. It will ignite and hopefully catch the sand particles on fire. We wait for a count of ten and then we charge. Everyone ready?"

Everyone was nodding that they understood.

Lila Zapata could feel her heart pounding in her chest as she cracked open the door. She watched as Lund activated and tossed a small cylindrical device onto the roof. He and Zapata pulled the door shut. The thermite device detonated on the roof top. The flames caught the smaller purple sand particles and a chain reaction occurred. The entire roof top erupted into a small fireball. It lasted for only a few seconds as the sands susceptible to fire burned out. Montrose was temporarily blinded and he suffered some burns on his outer clothing and his hair. Junior was scorched by the flames on his face and clothing.

Zapata held the door handle with both hands. They all counted to ten and she swung the door open. The cadets each rushed through the door; Dino Black was first, followed by Lund and Hodges. The wind was howling and purple sand was swirling all around. Black stepped on a trip wire which sent stun and flame darts flying at the men following behind him. Black was hit by laser blasts from Montrose and Junior who were hiding behind solar cell storage blocks which gave the two men perfect cover. Most of the darts hit the walls and fell harmlessly to the rooftop.

One of the flame darts hit Hodges in the chest. Hodges screamed when he looked at the dart and recognized what it was by the orange and yellow color of the thin cylinder of the weapon. Before Hodges could react, a clear bubble enveloped him and the dart activated. Hodges last thoughts were that he regretted he did not take the time to go talk with the lovely Reynita Calderon. Even over the roar of the loud wind, the cadets could hear the horrible screams as Hodges was roasted alive by the flames. He was dead in seconds.

Two other cadets were also hit by the darts. They screamed in terror just before their lives were ended in a searing burst of flames. Their flesh and internal organs burned to ash in seconds. Several other cadets were dropped by stun darts. They slid to the metal roof and were in the same condition as Dominic Andolini.

The others were through the door and Gorski, Harrison, Evart, Brandon Harcourt and Lund were firing back. Lund had never lost a man in combat and kept his mind on the battle as there would be time for mourning later, if there was a later. The adversaries that they were facing were well trained and motivated.

After witnessing two of their fellow students and Hodges get burned alive, several of the cadets fled back down the stairs. The flame darts had some of the effect that Junior hoped which was to demoralize the cadets that had volunteered to help Gorski and his friends out. The numbers against them was now more manageable with the majority of the cadets losing their nerve.

One other cadet, Lila Zapata, picked up Hodges' dropped laser pistol. The flame darts and laser fire had not scared her off as it had many others. Although her breathing was out of control, she pushed herself to help out her fellow classmates. She had been able to check on Dino Black and another prone cadet and she found they were only stunned. The two men would have one hell of a headache when they woke up but they would live. Zapata returned fire at the two killers. She took cover behind a large solar panel and saw that Gorski and Harrison were moving forward. Firing, advancing, taking cover and firing again. Zapata was impressed by the precision that Gorski and Harrison exhibited as they closed in on the evil men. At the same time she was disgusted by the cadets that had turned tail and ran.

Junior fired back. His years of training had developed the skill to peak out from a safe spot, locate a target, fire upon him and then slide back behind the cover. Junior, using those skills, was able to locate a charging cadet and fire on him. Brandon Harcourt was hit and slid hard on the roof top. Montrose was also firing, using similar tactics. Montrose saw Evart moving from one solar panel to another and shot at him. Evart was hit and he slumped unconscious. Gorski and Harrison used the split seconds when Junior and Montrose would hide back behind their cover to their advantage and charged closer to the two killers. Zapata and Lund were also charging. As Zapata was running from one solar box to another, she was hit by a laser blast fired by Montrose and she spun down onto the roof, hitting it with a soft thud.

Montrose, who was standing as he fired his laser at Zapata, was hit by a shot from Gorski and he fell backwards to the ground. Junior began running toward one of the other exits. He and Montrose had wired the other three doors with explosives and flame darts to demoralize any other cadets that attempted to intervene on Gorski's behalf. Junior decided his best chance was to get off the roof top and fight his way back to the fifth floor, free Chang and Quintana, and finish the mission another time. Montrose was pretty much finished now and would be bound and gagged by the cadets. Junior's once handsome face was cut in several places from the caustic sand. He was running as fast as he could to the nearest emergency door when Harrison tackled him. Both Junior and Harrison fell to the roof top and rolled over each other.

Junior punched Harrison in the face, stunning him for just a second. Lund was almost on them, but Junior had maintained control of his weapon. Seeing Lund charging at him, Junior fired and hit Lund in the right shoulder, sending him sliding backward on the roof top. Harrison grabbed Junior's right wrist, and twisted it until he dropped his laser pistol. Gorski was there and placed Junior in a headlock. The two cadets took turns punching the assassin until he seemed to succumb to the brute force. Junior felt as if his head was going to explode from the pounding the two cadets were delivering. Gorski pinned him down, face first and used the arm bindings they had purchased from Giles Lancer to tie his arms behind his back. Harrison tied Junior's legs together at the ankles. Gorski searched the man and found knives, flame darts, stun darts and other weapons such as garrotes, a stiletto and an ice pick.

"Watch him!" Gorski barked as he rushed to where Montrose had fallen. Gorski secured Montrose's arms and legs just as they had done to Junior. Gorski realized only he and Harrison were left on the roof as everyone else was unconscious. Hodges and the two other dead cadets were reduced to smoking skeletons.

"What now?" Harrison asked as Gorski walked toward him.

"Lift that piece of poggie crap up!" Gorski barked.

Harrison grabbed Junior Ragnarsson by the neck and lifted him into the air. Harrison held the killer suspended off the ground, squeezing his neck.

"Who are you?" Harrison demanded.

Junior began laughing as he felt the situation he found himself in to be humorous. He was the first son of the greatest assassin in several solar systems. And here he was, being interrogated by two cadets that had a history of discipline problems. Never had he imagined that he would be defeated by such men. They were not professionals. He had been bested by mere amateurs.

"You should really let me go!" Junior warned them.

"What are you going to do about it?" Gorski challenged.

"It won't be me that will be getting revenge on you," Junior promised. "Let me go and I will make this all go away."

"Who killed our friend Drayton?" Gorski demanded.

"Go kiss my hairy ass!" Junior told them as he quickly realized that the Rosenburg's were correct to be concerned about Gorski. He was not going to let the murder of his friend go. "Your only chance to live a long life is to release me."

Gorski looked around thinking. He ignored the pain when pieces of sand would hit him. He ran over to Montrose and dragged the unconscious man over to where Harrison was holding Junior.

"I am guessing you were the leader!" Gorski yelled over the howling winds. Gorski pulled out a knife and cut the bindings off the legs and arms of Montrose. "You are going to talk to us you bastard. You hurt our friends. You killed Hodges and your employers killed our friend Dray. Start talking! Who killed Dray!"

"Fuck you!" Junior growled as Harrison's grip around his neck increased.

Gorski propped the unconscious Montrose on the wall. "Too bad your friend here tried to escape. He tripped over the wall. He might survive the fall of twenty-two floors up, but I highly doubt it."

Junior began laughing. He had studied Gorski's dossier and determined that Gorski was a carouser, a troublemaker and a great fighter, but Gorski had never killed anyone before. He continued to laugh. "You are no killer. You would not dare."

Gorski held Montrose up on the wall. He thought about what the assassin said, and he was correct. He was not a killer. Gorski was torn, he wanted to throw the killer over the wall to his death, but he felt wrong about it. Gorski began to wonder what his father would do in this same situation. Or his mother. He was certain that neither of his parents would drop this hired assassin to his death, no matter how much he deserved it.

Mark Lund was pushing himself to his feet as Gorski was struggling with his morality. The stun blast that had hit him was not a full charge which meant that the lasers of the enemy must have been losing their potency. Lund saw that Gorski and Harrison were trying to interrogate the assassin. Gorski had one of the killers on the wall. Lund understood immediately that Gorski was trying to show the other killer what would happen to him if he did not talk. Lund looked into Gorski's eyes and concluded that the cadet was unable to push himself to do what was necessary.

Lund walked over to the group, covering his eyes from the sands. He reached Gorski who seemed surprised he had recovered so quickly.

Lund turned his attention toward Junior, "Talk or die!"

Junior Ragnarsson responded by spitting at Lund. The assassin did not recognize Lund from the computer files he had studied regarding

Gorski's inner circle. He was at a loss as to how one of the Gorski Gang members would not have been in the computer system, if the mystery man was a member. He seemed too familiar with Gorski and Harrison; especially in the manner the two cadets seemed to show the man so much deference.

There needed to be vengeance for the killing of Private First Class Bill Hodges, Lund thought to himself, as well as the two eighteen year old cadets that died on the roof. Lund decided to take action. He walked over to Gorski and took Montrose from his hands. Lund leaned Montrose over the edge of the wall, hoping that by demonstrating an act of deplorable cruelty, he would convince the other assassin to start talking. He paused for a few seconds for dramatic effect and then flung Montrose over the wall to his death. Due to the loud winds, no one heard the crushing thump on the pavement below when Montrose's fall from twenty-two floors up came to a crashing end.

Junior took in a deep breath as the mystery man proved that he had the guts to act decisively. These men were capable of killing after all. Junior was furious because they just murdered Montrose, one of his most trusted men and a dear friend. No one does that to the Ragnarsson's he thought. The reality was that Junior Ragnarsson and each of the mercenaries that worked with him had all contemplated that one day a mission could go wrong. That day had arrived. He had never revealed his fears of dying to anyone else as he had concerns that showing fear would make him come across as weak.   Harrison slammed him to the ground, knocking the breath out of him.

"Talk or die!" Harrison screamed into his face.

"Let's get everyone inside!" Lund said loudly over the winds. "We have two more of his friends downstairs. I am going to take pleasure in skinning them all alive."

The three men noticed that Li Mingjuan, Maria Haake and some other female cadets had made their way to the rooftop and were carrying their unconscious friends into the stairwell and away from the howling winds and the harmful sands. Black, Zapata and Brandon Harcourt would wake up with a splitting headache, but they would be alive.

Lund whispered to Gorski as they watched the others being cared for, "In combat, sometimes you need to get damn mean. Next time, kill the hostage. Other than that, you and Harrison kicked some ass tonight."

Lund picked up the bound and bleeding Junior Ragnarsson and threw him over his shoulder. "Let's go have a conversation downstairs."

Harrison used his holo-com and contacted the group of cadets on the fifth floor to come upstairs to help with the others that were unconscious. Once everyone had been removed from the roof, Harrison slammed the door shut. He leaned against the wall. He had really liked Hodges and had hoped to get to know the man better. Harrison was glad that Lund threw the one killer over the wall. He was looking forward to the others receiving similar swift deaths.

Junior Ragnarsson did not struggle as Harrison dragged him down the stairs. He had been beaten by the upstart cadets which meant that

Father would be very, very upset.

CHAPTER NINE

Using a stolen security card, Ivar Ragnarsson was able to get Emma and Dulce Ragnarsson into the women's dormitory. The protective barricades were closing soon after as the Lock Down was initiated. The three had their orders which seemed simplistic enough. Capture the two women and get them aboard the Raumschiff for transport back to Rosenburg's Ranch.

The three observed the Recreation Center on the first floor of the dormitory. It was bustling with activity. There were hundreds of female cadets laughing and playing various three dimensional holographic computer games. Other women were playing simpler games from the past such as pool and shuffle board. The ratio of women to men in the dormitory was about five to one.

Ivar leaned in close to his sister, Emma, "Sis, it is so easy to hook up here."

"Really little brother?" Emma responded disapprovingly. "You were sent her to become an officer in the Space Command. Chasing cheap women will get you nowhere. Remember that father has big plans for you and I am sure they do not include these cheap sluts."

Dulce seemed unimpressed with the conversation. She was watching the activity around them, students playing the three dimensional computer war games, competing at chess, pool, shuffle board and other games. She saw two of the female cadets fondling and kissing each another on top of one of the pool tables. Dulce ignored the display of public affection and kept looking around the area in search of their two cadets. She was disappointed that she did not locate their two targets in the huge lobby area. She motioned to Ivar, who was watching the lesbian women start to undress on the pool table and to Emma to follow her up the stairs. There were men and women making comments about the storm coming their way as the assassins walked past them. Dulce walked around the students and then rapidly ascended the stairs. Ivar and Emma were keeping pace with her; Ivar was asking what the hurry was when he wanted to watch the two girls on the pool table.

Dulce had been born with the name Dulce Maria Reynolds Hernandez. When she had been a young girl, her grandparents abandoned her to the Rosenburg family as partial payment of a debt. Her other brothers and sisters were also given to the cruel and immoral Rosenburg family. Dulce found out the hard way to never cross her owners. Her first lesson in the cruelty of the Rosenburg family was when her older brother attempted to escape after their first week of slavery. When he was caught, he was fed to some slithering creatures at the Arena. The Rosenburg's forced Dulce and her siblings to watch as their older brother was ripped to pieces and devoured. That event hardened Dulce, changed her from a sweet little girl with dreams of a career in medicine and to one day have a husband and family. She decided she would do whatever it took to survive in her new horror filled environment.

When she was a teenager, she was told to live with her current husband, Junior. He had found her desirable and negotiated with the Rosenburg's for her to be transferred over to him. She had been payment for a job he finished for the Rosenburg family. At age fourteen, she was married off to the killer. He had several other wives, but he seemed to prefer the company of Dulce over all of the others. He taught her how to fight, defend herself and how to kill another human being with ruthless efficiency. Despite her indoctrination into the world of killing without emotion, Dulce always hoped to have the opportunity to escape him and free her siblings, wherever they were. She had no love for the cruel man that was her husband and pretended to enjoy his company as a survival method. Her one desire was to seek out her family that had lost her all those years ago.

But for today, Dulce Maria Reynolds Hernandez Ragnarsson had to help kidnap two women that had wronged the Rosenburg's in some way. She did not wish to be a part of the mission, but to refuse would mean punishment for her. It could come in the form of no food for a few days or whippings or even execution. Dulce knew that the two women would most likely suffer horrible fates once they were delivered to the Rosenburg family. Although she felt sympathy for the two girls, Dulce would be the loyal soldier so that one day she would have the opportunity to flee.

She made her way through a sea of female cadets running around in their underwear, passing liquor bottles back and forth, onto the floor where the woman Jen Staszko lived. There were more women dancing in the halls, loud music playing. Some men were present, kissing some of the women, others dancing to the music. Others were merely engaged in conversation. As she led Emma and Ivar through the gauntlet of women and men in the hallway, one female cadet grabbed Ivar by the arm and started kissing him. Emma pushed the female away from her brother and grabbed him by the arm to keep him moving. The female cadet screamed a string of curse words at Emma.

Jen Staszko's dormitory room was at the end of the hallway a fact that Dulce had memorized as she prepared for the mission. Dulce stopped at the door and pulled out of her pocket a hand sized computer that hacked into the dormitory security system in less than ten seconds. She ordered the door opened and watched as it slid open. The three Ragnarsson's moved into the room quickly and the door slid shut behind them. Dulce and Emma had laser pistols drawn and ready. Ivar stood at the doorway as the women searched the room from top to bottom.

It was empty.

Next door, Jen Staszko and Elektra Papanikolaou were sitting with their shadows, Sara Stewart and LaShondra Lewis, watching their computer screen that showed the two women and the lone man searching their dormitory room.

"There they are, just three of them," Stewart observed with a whisper.

Papanikolaou was looking at their faces closely, to see if she recognized any of them. "They are not the ones that killed Dray. The man in the background, I have seen him before. I think he is a student here."

"We will know soon enough," Lewis told them as she gave a last second look at her laser pistol. "Their faces have all been downloaded to the central computer system at the Military Intelligence. If there is a match, we will know it soon. Should we pay them a visit?"

"Yes, please," Staszko said. She was in the mood for some revenge over the attempted rape of Elektra, the murder of Drayton and all the innocent people on the transport flight. She had her knives ready.

The four women stood up from their chairs and moved toward the door. They had previously agreed that the best way to handle the situation was to trap the three attackers in the room, stun them and then begin the interrogations. Lewis took the lead and pushed open the door. She drew her laser pistol and held it in her right hand as she walked toward the other dormitory room.

Emma Ragnarsson had her laser pistol ready as she cursed to herself that none of the targets were in the room. She was surprised when she heard the door open and turned to see who was coming in. Lewis moved into the room quickly looking this way and that for someone to shoot at. Emma did not recognize Lewis from any of the files she studied for the mission. Emma immediately fired her laser and Lewis took the blast in her abdomen, sending her to her knees and then face first to the ground. Emma quickly concluded that they had been set up when she noticed that Lewis dropped a laser pistol to the carpeted floor. It was as if these women knew that someone was in Staszko's room. Emma tried to aim at the next woman but she was not fast enough.

Stewart fired her laser pistol at Emma and hit her in the chest. Emma felt the electrical current surge in her body, she screamed and she fell to the floor.

Dulce dived behind the furthest bed from the door. Ivar tried to pull out his laser pistol as he saw Staszko and Papanikolaou storm the room. Before he could get the laser out, Staszko had wrapped her arms around him and put a knife to his throat.

Stewart was firing at Dulce and Dulce fired back. Papanikolaou was astonished that both Stewart and Dulce stunned each other at the same time. They both slumped to the floor, their weapons sliding from their limp hands. "Bind them!" Staszko hissed. She pushed the man onto the bed, keeping her knife at his throat. The man was crying and begging for his life. Staszko waited as Elektra tied up their two would-be female attackers. Once it was done, Staszko turned her attention to the man. He was breathing heavily out of fear and he was perspiring.

Ivar did not want to die. By the way they were moving, these women meant business. He had to find a way out of his current predicament. His eyes were darting back and forth watching Staszko's every move.

The Greek woman pulled out a knife and approached him, "You better start talking, or by Hera I will cut out your heart."

"Wait, wait!" Ivar pleaded. "I am a student here! These two girls just asked me to show them around. I don't know them!"

Staszko knew that he was not being completely truthful by the look in his eyes. Her former life as s gypsy taught her to be able to assess the veracity of people by looking at their faces and observing their body language. His gave toward the floor and slumping shoulders indicated that he had something to hide. "Computer, identify the man in my dorm room."

"His name is Ivar Ragnarsson, cadet freshman, Clovis Academy," the computer responded.

"So he is telling part of the truth," Elektra said softly. "I think he knows a lot more than he is saying. I say we cut of his balls."

"No!" Ivar protested. "Please. Don't hurt me!"

"You better start giving us answers you little slime ball." Staszko made the tip of her knife nick the skin on the man's neck, drawing blood.

Ivar cried out in pain and urinated his pants. He was certain these women were going to kill him based on the fact that Elektra had killed Daryl Rosenburg and Staszko had injured one or more of Caine's friends. "No! I don't want to die. Please."

Elektra could smell the urine and tried hard not to gag on the smell.

"You want to live? Then tell me the names of the men that tried to rape me and the men that murdered our friend! I want names you little cretin!"

"I don't know!" Ivar lied. "Please. I know nothing of any rape or murder. All I know is these two girls asked me to take them to the women's dormitory."

"Explain why you followed them to my room!" Staszko slightly cut his cheek, causing immediate pain for the lad but not drawing much blood.

"They promised me sex!" Ivar cried out. "I thought I was going to get laid."

"Then why were you holding an illegal laser pistol?" Staszko hissed into his ear. "You came here to kill me and my friend. But, tonight, you will die instead." Staszko quickly stabbed a stun dart into Ivar's neck. He cried out, fell limp onto the bed and found that he could not move. He felt paralyzed. He could hear and see everything around him, but his muscles were not responding. Staszko pushed him off the bed and on the floor.

"He is a liar," Elektra concluded. She was holding her left hand over her mouth and nose due to Ivar wetting himself.

"Yes he is," Staszko agreed. "I think you were correct. We should cut off his balls. Help me drag him into the bathtub. We can slice him up and wash the blood down the drain."

Ivar could not protest as the women dragged him across the floor and to the restroom. The two women, using their knives, cut off all of his clothing and taunted him as they did so. Once Ivar was completely nude, the two women rolled him into the bathtub. He was crying and terrified, hoping his sister would wake up and help him. He wished he had just told the two women the truth when he could have. With the venom of the stun dart in his veins, he could not speak at all.

He could hear Elektra reviving the other two women and watched the dark skinned woman, Lewis, enter the restroom and gaze down at him.

"What should we do with them?" Staszko asked Lewis. "I say we cut his balls off in front of the two women and get him to talk."

"We should wake them up," Lewis said as she was thinking of a plan. "Perhaps watching the male in their group being tortured will loosen their lips."

"I'll take care of it," Stewart volunteered.

The military undercover women had brought an ample supply of smelling salts to wake up any person that had been hit by a stun laser. Stewart first revived the bound Emma and then Dulce. Stewart and Lewis dragged the two women to the bathroom and set them on stools, facing the bathtub.

Emma was still delirious from the laser blast, her head pounding and her mouth was dry from the effects of the laser. She was forcing herself to concentrate, just as her father had trained her to do. He instructed her that there will always be an opportunity to escape as long as you look for the chance like an eagle. She saw that her brother was naked in the bathtub and crying like a baby. His legs and arms were bound just as hers and Dulce's were. Dulce was silent and showing no emotion. Emma noticed that Jen Staszko was holding a razor sharp knife; the blade was about a foot long.   From reading the reports of what happened on the space station, Emma was aware that Staszko knew how to use a knife from what happened to Chin.

"Now," Staszko said with authority, "everyone is awake. My friend Elektra and I have many questions for you ladies. We have questioned your man here, and he told us some things. But we have some, shall we say, fill in the blanks questions. If I am not satisfied with your answers, I will start cutting him. I will slice off his flesh, piece by piece, whenever you lie to me. I will cut off his balls. After I cut off his balls I will force both you ladies to eat one."

Stasko put her knife pointing at Ivar's crotch, "Now. Who were the men that tried to rape Elektra and killed Drayton?"

"I know nothing of such accusations," Dulce said calmly and quickly.

"How about you?" Lewis asked, pointing at Emma Ragnarsson.

"I never heard of such things," Emma lied softly. She knew the situation was going from bad to worse. If Ivar lost his family jewels, father would be furious. If Emma or Ivar told all they knew to save Ivar's family jewels, father and the Rosenburg family would feed them to their animals in the Arena. Either way, there was no happy ending for them to the situation.

Dulce was contemplating her options. She wondered if these four women could help her escape her psychotic husband and his family. If Dulce told them all she knew, would they be able to protect her? Where would she go to live? Would they be able to help her free her surviving siblings? And, if she talked, what if Junior had already succeeded in his mission to capture Gorski and Evart? It would only be a matter of time before he came for the women. Talking carried too many risks, Dulce decided, unless they made an offer that would ensure her safety.

Staszko shook her head at Emma, "Wrong answer ladies."

Emma watched helplessly as Staszko sliced into Ivar's right leg and cut off about a two inch chunk of flesh. Ivar could not scream, due to the stun dart. The sensation of pain was excruciating. Staszko took the chunk of leg flesh and stuffed it into Emma's mouth.

"Chew it and swallow!" Staszko ordered.

Emma spit the piece of human flesh out of her mouth. "Bitch! You touch any of the three of us again and you will die!"

Lewis laughed at the empty threat, "Really? In case you have not noticed, we are not the ones tied up. You are the ones that are in danger now. You three walked right into it. Now, do we continue cutting your man to pieces or do you talk? Make a decision!"

Emma said nothing. She looked down at her feet, but Stewart grabbed her chin and forced her head up to watch. Staszko sliced off another inch and a half of Ivar's skin, this time she took it from his left knee cap. Stasko tossed the bloody chunk of flesh at Emma's face. Ivar had an involuntary bowel movement due to the pain and fear. His feces spread on the bottom of the bath tub. Staszko turned on the tub water spout to wash the feces chunks down the drain.

"He is really scared," Elektra said in Dulce's ear. "When your friends tried to rape me, I was never so frightened. I am so glad you three are here so I can get some payback."

Dulce said nothing and watched as Staszko began shaving Ivar's head with her long knife. Staszko cut into his scalp as she worked. She took several hands full of hair and threw it in the faces of Emma and Dulce. Staszko left small patches of hair on the man's head, but the skull was bare and bleeding in several places. If Ivar survived, he would not be able to show his face again for a week or two.

Lewis sighed, "Jen, these bitches are not going to talk. Cut off his balls and let's force them to eat his testicles. Let him bleed out in the bathtub and then we kill the women."

Staszko shrugged, "Okay." She placed the blade of her knife on Ivar's right testicle and began to press it into his flesh.

"Stop!" Emma yelled, worried of her father's wrath if she allowed one of his sons to be castrated. "I will tell you all you want to know."

Staszko kept the knife at Ivar's groin and glared at Emma, "Who tried to rape Elektra and what are the names of the men that killed Drayton?"

Emma's father had spent considerable time teaching her how to lie to others effectively. She decided to use the names of some people that she and her family had killed in the past. "Stephen Miller was the leader. His little brother Anthony was there and your friend killed him when she stabbed him. The other person was named Harvey Rose. Those were the only names I know. The others I never met, I don't know their names."

"Computer," Jen Staszko said, sensing that she was being lied to. "Run the names Stephen and Anthony Miller and Harvey Rose. Any matches of those three names being used together in any reports?"

"Stephen and Anthony Miller were killed with their family on the Martian colonies two years ago by unknown assassins. The entire family of six was found dead. There are several matches for a Harvey Rose, but none of the Harvey Rose individuals have crossed paths with the Miller's." The computer ended its' report.

"Lying tramp," Staszko shook her head and waived her knife blade in Emma's direction.

"If we tell you anything we are dead!" Emma protested.

"Well, you will all die right here, tonight, unless you speak," Lewis said. "Last chance."

Emma knew she had given it her best shot to try and save Ivar. But these women were going to stop at nothing to get the truth. Her father would kill her if she talked. In her molar was a tablet that her father placed in all of his hired assassins, even his children. The tablet was an advanced mixture of cyanide and acid. The acid was a type found on a giant planet, of mostly gas, but it had rivers of acid. Just two drops of that acid would dissolve the entire body of a human in sixty seconds. Father had paid considerable sums of money to dental experts to make a compound tablet of cyanide and the deadly acid. Dell Ragnarsson had many reasons to require all of his employees and family to have the death tablet implanted in their teeth. The main justification for the dental implant was to avoid talking or, more specifically, avoid being forced to talk. The cyanide would cause a swift death and the acid would ensure nothing was left of the body for DNA testing. Emma did not wish to die, but she began contemplating the use of her suicide pill as a death by cyanide would be preferable to the certain torture father would inflict on them all. Ivar had a pill similar to Emma's in his mouth. But, due to the stun dart, he was unable to use it.

"Ladies, a word?" Stewart motioned for Lewis, Staszko and Elektra to step out of the bath room and into the main bedroom.

The four women left the Ragnarsson's in the rest room. Stewart had been recording the entire interrogation on her Holo-com device and had the entire feed being routed into the main satellites to the MI headquarters for analysis. Stewart left her device in the restroom in the hopes the three would-be assassins would speak when they were left alone together.

"I have some Anhalidia biocormidine," Stewart told them with a tint of pride in her voice.

"What is that?" Elektra asked as she had never heard of the term before.

"Truth serum, highly concentrated," Lewis answered for Stewart. "Okay that might make things go faster. Get it ready."

"But," Staszko began, "if we do not show the same ruthlessness to them as they did to Drayton and the innocents on the Transport, then they will just keep on coming after us. We need to send them a message."

"By cutting of a man's penis?" Stewart asked. "Get real. We have to abide by the laws. We are not the criminals here, Jen. They are. We will send a message to the bad guys."

"How?" Staszko crossed her arms.

"By indicting and prosecuting these heathens," Lewis said.

Staszko took in that statement and frowned. Lewis seemed to have every faith in the legal system. Staszko did not share her optimism. From her perspective, the law seemed to favor the rich and the powerful. Staszko and her family had many altercations of the years against the wealthy and politically connected. Staszko's family always came out with the short end of the stick.

"All right, LaShondra, we do it your way," Staszko gave in. "But for the record, I believe you are being naive. We should kill them all and not give them any opportunity to bribe some corrupt Judge or politician. The world is not as fair and just as you may believe."

In the bathroom, Emma was whispering instructions to Dulce and Ivar, "Tell them nothing. My father will kill us in ways so horrible that you cannot imagine."

"I was forced into this ill-advised plan," Dulce reminded her. "If I stay silent, will I get my freedom? Will I ever get to see my mother or father again? You people fed one of my brothers to those monsters years ago. What happened to all of my other siblings? What did your sick family do to all of them? Why should I have any loyalty to you?"

Emma glared at Dulce, "You will do it because they can still feed the rest of your family to those meat eating monsters. You will do it because we will not hesitate to kill our own to maintain order. Am I clear on that?"

"Promise me my freedom and I will keep silent," Dulce told Emma. "I want to go back home to my parents."

"I promise, when we get out of this I will get my brother to release you," Emma lied. The truth was she would advocate to her brother Dell to feed Dulce to the creatures. Dulce was no longer trustworthy and needed to be eliminated.

The four women re-entered the bathroom. Without warning, Lewis took a firm hold of Emma's left arm and Stewart injected a clear, light blue fluid into her. Emma Ragnarsson knew immediately what it was: truth serum.

"No!" Emma yelled in fear.

The capsule in her tooth was sensitive to any form of truth serum entering the blood stream. The injection would trigger the cyanide liquid acid implant. She felt herself losing control as the serum was overtaking her. Within two minutes of receiving the injection, the capsule in Emma's mouth burst open. She fell backwards in her stool, foaming at the mouth. Her eyes were rolling back as her body was shaking and convulsing. The acid entered her blood stream and permeated her flesh, muscle and bone.

The cyanide worked its' deadly roll quickly and then the acid took effect. Lewis, Stewart, Elektra and Staszko watched in horror as Emma's body began to decay before their eyes. Her skin shriveled and her eyes became sunken. Her hair began to vaporize as the flesh on her body was melting and her bones and internal organs dissolved before the four women could react. In seconds, there was nothing left of the body of Emma Ragnarsson. She had been completely consumed by the deadly acid.

"Holy Hera!" Elektra stepped backwards from the white smoke that was in the air where there had once been Emma Ragnarsson.

All that remained of Emma was a small layer of white ashes which were fading away.

"Now can I castrate him?" Staszko asked, pointing her knife at Ivar Ragnarsson.

There was silence until Dulce Ragnarsson spoke up, "You activated the liquid cyanide and acid from the gas planet Luft. The acid is quite lethal and as you saw, it works in seconds. The mixture is embedded in each of us, in our teeth, and will react if we are injected with truth serum. You ladies killed her."

"Are you ready to talk, or do I inject you with truth serum next?" Stewart asked in a threatening tone.

"I need protection," Dulce told them calmly. "If you can get someone with authority to give me protection, amnesty and immunity from prosecution, I have a story for you that will rock your world. And you had better get a good dentist to remove my molar because I have one of those ticking time bombs in my mouth, too."

Dulce paused and looked at Ivar Ragnarsson, whose eyes were wide with fear. "And go ahead and castrate him. I hate his whole family."

"Okay," Staszko began moving toward Ivar with the knife. Stewart put her hand on her arm to stop her.

"Cool it for a moment. Let's take this young lady into the next room," Stewart advised. They all helped Dulce into the next room, set her on a bed and closed the door to the bathroom, leaving Ivar in the bathtub next to the small pile of ashy remains of her older sister.

"Start talking," Lewis said impatiently.

"Not til I have a deal in writing giving me immunity, protection and amnesty," Dulce told the women.

"It may take some time," Stewart informed her.

"I promise, I will make it worth the wait," Dulce said with confidence. "And you two, Elektra and Jen, when my story gets out no one will ever screw with you again."

CHAPTER TEN

Lester Brey Gillis had been transported to the Cordell Hull United Nations Hospital along with his shadow, Corporal Frank Preston, Yesenia Guevara and William Bragg. During the brawl between Gillis and Bragg, both men suffered some bruising and other possible injuries. Bragg was unconscious, but breathing and stable. His blood pressure was low and the computer scans indicated the possibility of some internal bleeding. Guevara stayed by his side, holding her child in her arms. The flight to the hospital had been rough due to the high winds whipping around the emergency transport ship.

The sand storm had been growing progressively worse and the Lock Down had been initiated by the Clovis City climatologists. Emergency Medical Technicians at the hospital rushed out to the transportation glider and carried Bragg out on a stretcher. Gillis was placed on a wheel chair by a nurse and wheeled into the hospital. Bragg had fallen to the pavement face first, so the medical staff determined he should be assessed for any blunt force trauma or concussion.

Gillis was taken to an elevator and to the radiology unit to have x-rays of his ribs, arms, clavicle and hands for possible breaks. Preston went with Gillis, refusing to leave his side. Preston was certain that no hit team would find them at the hospital, but he was not going to let his guard down. The hospital had little in the way of manned security. If a team of assassins attacked them here, they would be essentially on their own.

A doctor met the two men at the X-Ray floor. She was an attractive blonde and it seemed like her approach was no nonsense. She immediately recognized Gillis.

"Les Gillis," Doctor Freya Doernitz Cardenas said. "What kind of trouble did you get into today?"

Cardenas was a close friend of Sophia DuBravac. Based on that relationship, Freya and Porfirio Cardenas had gone on several 'double dates' with Gillis and DuBravac. Freya liked Gillis and had always felt he and DuBravac made a good couple.

"A fight," Gillis told her simply. "You should see the other guy."

Freya nodded at his answer. Nothing had changed with the hot-headed Irishman. Freya constantly defended Gillis when her husband would criticize the brawls that seemed to always have Gillis in the middle of the action. Freya believed that the man would mature in time. The doctor had also implored DuBravac to have a little more patience with Gillis, especially when her ultimatum did not go as she had expected and decided it was time to move on.

"And you are?" Freya directed her question at Preston.

"Frank Preston, ma'am. I am with Military Intelligence and assigned to protect Mister Gillis." He introduced himself while shaking her hand.

"Okay, Frank Preston from Military Intelligence, I am Doctor Cardenas. I will need you to wait here while we get a battery of x-rays on Les here."

"Ma'am, are there any other entrances to this floor other than the elevator we came up in and those emergency stairs over there?" Preston was pointing down the hallway.

"That is it, Mr. Preston," she affirmed. "When we go to Lock Down, only the hospital emergency metal doors at the lower level will allow entrance on the premises. We will be quite safe."

"Thank you, doctor."

Freya felt the man was being a little over protective of Gillis. She never knew that Gillis was a celebrity in need of a body guard. Gillis was wheeled away by an orderly to another room for the recommended x-rays.

"Protection?" Freya mumbled to herself. "What in the world did you do this time, Les Gillis?" She determined she would contact Sophia DuBravac and see if she knew what her former lover had gotten himself into. With the Gorski Gang, there was no telling.

William Bragg was placed in a triple bed overnight room with another patient. Yesenia Guevara sat in a chair next to her husband's bed, holding her son close to her. The other patient was asleep in the second bed. The third bed was empty. Bragg had been treated by Dr. Harding, the resident head trauma specialist, and she found that there had been no trauma to the brain. Bragg was given an injection for pain. Dr. Harding instructed Guevara to allow Bragg time for sleep.

Guevara reflected on the past few days' events. Her true love had died. According to Gillis, he had been murdered in cold blood. She was frequently abused by her current husband and he even killed her pet in an effort to exert control over her. Guevara wondered what her mental issue was that caused her to keep going back to Bragg and suffering more abuse. She thought about what the best course of action for her and her son would be concluded that she should pack up and leave Bragg behind. She feared his reprisal from Gillis' unannounced visit to the home. Her biggest fear was that her son would grow up seeing the family violence and think that it was normal. She did not want her child to grow up and believe that hitting a woman was proper behavior. She wanted him to have a good man to be a role model for him and Bragg had proven by his actions to be a terrible example of what a man should be. Guevara decided that she would not be at the home when Bragg was released. She was ready to leave him for good.

After some time had passed, Guevara and her son fell asleep in the room.

Gillis dressed after the pictures of his bone structure had been completed. He was instructed to wait in the lobby for the radiologist technician.

Gillis found that Frank Preston was there, waiting for him.

"How do you feel?"

"I feel great," Gillis sat down next to the man that was serving as his body guard. "Any news from the others?"

Preston had his palm holo-com in his right hand, "I have tried to raise Sergeant First Class Lund and get no response. That is not like him."

"And the girls?" Gillis was worried about his friends.

"No response from agents Lewis or Stewart either."

"The sand storm has some electrical magnetic qualities. Perhaps the connections for the broadcast network and the satellite system are experiencing some interference."

Preston nodded and recalled being told before the mission began that Gillis was some kind of genius.

"Can you try contacting someone else?" Gillis suggested. "Someone not at the Academy Dormitory. I'll do the same."

Both men began attempting to contact others. Gillis walked to the observation windows and saw that the protective metal barricades had already been secured to protect the hospital from the strong winds. He asked his communication device to connect him, person to person, with Penelope Smith. To Gillis' pleasant surprise, she answered.

"This is Penelope."

"This is Les. How are you tonight?"

Penelope Rosenburg smiled at the sound of his voice, "I am doing well. Drinking a glass of merlot and relaxing in my suite at the Hotel. How are you?"

"I am doing fine. My classmates and I are hoping this sand storm passes us by with little to no damage," Gillis told her.

"I saw the news," Penelope was lying on her bed in her personal suite at the Hotel Baroness. She had just showered and was wearing a bathrobe and enjoying her bottle of wine. "Too bad you did not come up here to the space station. We could have watched the storm system from one of the five star restaurants and enjoyed each other's company."

"That would have been a divine way to ride the storm out," Gillis told her. "How was work today?"

"Uneventful. Boring." She poured herself another glass of wine. "Fortunately no dignitaries that I had to pretend to like and show around the station. I would really like to see you again."

"I would like that as well," Gillis saw that Preston was approaching him. "Perhaps we can plan for something this weekend. Why don't you and I take a trip together?"

"Where to?"

"Let me surprise you," Gillis suggested.

"All right, man of mystery. Surprise me."

"I will contact you again tomorrow."

Penelope wanted to continue the conversation with Gillis, but was certain she needed to get some rest. She was glad that Ella's brother had not caught up to the handsome cadet. "Til tomorrow, Les Gillis. Watch yourself in the storm."

"Good night," Gillis closed his holo-com. He hated ending the conversation, but Preston had something on his mind. "Any news, Frank?"

"I was able to reach a friend of mine at the U.N. Headquarters and she answered. The broadcast network is fine. That would mean my fellow M.I. undercover mates are busy."

Gillis was about to say something when he heard his name called out. He and Preston turned to see and attractive strawberry-blonde woman, her long hair pulled back into a pony-tail and her light brown eyes were revealing that she was happy to see Gillis. She was smiling at the men, showing a set of perfect teeth. She was in a baby blue one-piece doctor's uniform and holding a folder. Gillis knew immediately who she was and walked over to her and hugged her.

"Julia Steiner! You look ravishing!" Gillis greeted her. She looked radiant and happy. It had been several weeks since Gillis had seen Steiner. Of all the Gorski Gang members, Julia Steiner had been his favorite member. She was extremely smart, well read, spoke several languages, friendly, kind, generous and an exceptional scientific intellectual.

"Guten abend, Les," Steiner said as they hugged. "I never would have expected you to be here on this night of wild weather."

"Well, I got into a bit of a scuffle."

"Yes, I saw your charts," Steiner opened the file and there were pages of computer prints from the results. "I am happy to report you only have a few bruises. No broken bones."

"That is a relief," Gillis placed his holo-com device in his pocket. "What brings you here to the hospital?"

"My internship for my degree," Steiner said simply. "I have been training in the radiology section this week, last week in pediatrics. Next week I will start learning medications in the pharmacy section. How is everyone dealing with what happened to Dray?"

"Not well. It is a long story. Do you have time for a coffee?" Gillis suggested.

"I can take a break in an hour," Steiner said. "And with the Lock Down, you won't be going anywhere. I will meet you in the basement where the hospital cafeteria is located. I want to hear everything, Les." She touched Gillis' cheek with her hand and hugged him.

"In an hour," Gillis confirmed as she walked back to the duty station.

"What is it with you and the women?" Preston demanded.

"I just have many friends," Gillis shrugged. "Well, I have no broken bones. So, I am free to leave. But, with the Lock Down, I am not free to leave. Quite the dilemma."

"May I suggest we continue to attempt contact with the others?" Preston said.

"Certainly," Gillis began walking toward the stairs. "Let's check in on Will Bragg. Hopefully he is doing well."

"Why would you want to go see him after the melee you two had?"

"To kill time and maybe he will give me an excuse to kick his damn ass.”

With great effort, Nikko and Prescott made it to the Hospital. They were breathing heavily from their sprint from the dormitory to the medical building. The two men observed that the massive metallic doors had already been lowered to protect the hospital windows, walls and structure from the powerful winds. They ran around the perimeter of the building, covering their eyes from the sand and wind. Both men had some cuts on their faces from the sand.

Nikko began instructing his hand held Holo-com to hack into the Cordell Hull United Nations Hospital system. It took a few moments for his holo-com to begin blinking green to signify that it had gained entry to the Hospital Security system.

“We’re in!” Nikko yelled to Prescott over the howl of the winds. Nikko asked his device to open the security entrance to the Hospital. The two hired mercenaries waited for a few seconds until the doors began to slide open. They darted inside to escape the elements.

Nikko watched the doors as the slid shut behind them. He and Prescott were dusting themselves off in the hallway as a male doctor and two female nurses approached them.

“How did you two get in here?” The Doctor demanded. “Only a proper security code can open the emergency doors. I need to see some identification.”

Prescott and Nikko responded by pulling their hand lasers out and fired at the three hospital employees. They fell to the ground, stunned by the laser blasts. The two assassins dragged the three to the nearest restroom and tossed them inside.

"Security cameras are everywhere," Prescott observed. "If they are monitoring they will be on us quickly."

Nikko nodded holding up his palm computer device, "I am hacked into the hospital computer system already. Gillis checked in and was sent for x-rays and released. He came in with another man named William Bragg."

"Maybe he is with this Bragg fellow," Prescott speculated.

"Let's go see," Nikko agreed as he undressed the male doctor and began putting on the medical uniform for himself. As Nikko was dressing up as a doctor, he saw Prescott fondling the two unconscious nurses. "Hey, we don't have time for that."

"Sure we do. That sand storm will be churning things up for the next ten to twelve hours." Prescott had his hands running all over the body of one of the nurses. "This one here feels like she has a great set of tits."

"Leave them," Nikko ordered. Prescott was always the one on the team that would go too far. He was hard to control sometimes as he had his own way of doing things. Nikko did not like the fact that Junior had paired him off with Prescott. "Let's bag Gillis and then you can come back and do whatever you want with her. We have work to do you Limey shit."

"No racial slurs," Prescott began binding the three medical staff with plastic cords. "Okay, let's do what we came here for and then, that one there is all mine."

The two men walked cautiously out of the restroom. Prescott placed an "Out of Service" sign on the door as they left. The men found the elevator and rode it up to the third floor to where William Bragg was sleeping.

Upon arriving on the third floor, Nikko and Prescott began walking down the hallways searching for Bragg's room number. Nikko cursed under his breath as he found that the hallways were like a never ending maze of confusion.

"Help me," Nikko and Prescott heard a female voice behind them.

The two hired killers turned to see a female patient, leaning against the wall, struggling to stay upright. "Help me. Where am I?" She continued to repeat the phrase. Nikko and Prescott knew that was always the danger of wearing doctors' uniforms in a hospital. Some patient might actually demand help. Nikko decided to defuse the situation quickly. He walked over to the woman and fired his hand laser into her abdomen at point blank range. He caught her in his arms as she collapsed and carried her to the nearest room and laid her down on the floor.

Nikko heard some voices outside the room. At least two people were confronting Prescott. Nikko grunted to himself as he knew Prescott had a fiery temper. This mission was not going to be as easy as he had hoped. He walked out into the hallway and saw a female doctor named Harding and two male nurses with her. They were demanding to know Prescott's name and which patient he was looking for. Prescott pulled his hand laser and began firing, stunning the men.

"Alert!" Doctor Harding screamed just before Prescott stunned her. Nikko ran into the hallway, "Damn it, now you've done it!"

A nurse at the duty station hit the alarm. Red lights began flashing all over the hospital and a computer voice was warning everyone that there was an intruder alert in progress. Security guards that had been asleep on duty in their basement offices woke up and were grabbing hand lasers to begin a search for the unauthorized persons.

Nikko and Prescott switched their laser pistol settings to vaporize. They began firing into the security cameras on the ceiling, to keep the hospital security blinded. A male nurse charged at the two mercenaries, holding a metal bed pan over his head to use as a weapon. Prescott fired on the hospital employee and took pleasure in watching the deadly laser slowly burn him into a pile of grey ashes. The bed pan clanged to the floor as the arms holding it had been eliminated, as if the nurse had never existed. He did not even have time to scream as he died.

Yesenia Guevara woke up when she heard the alarms sounding. When Les Gillis had stopped by to visit them, he did not have the heart to wake here up and left for the cafeteria. She shook her husband awake. William Bragg was blinking his eyes, confused.

"Baby, get up!" Guevara urged as she lifted him into a sitting position. "Something bad is happening. Get up."

Bragg slowly rose to his feet, shaking his head. He tore the IV needle in his right arm out. He began moving toward the door looking all around him to get used to the environment he found himself in. He deduced that he was in a hospital due to the injuries he sustained from his fight with Gillis. Bragg had only one thought, he was going to find Gillis and kill him. He would deal with his disloyal wife after.

Guevara picked up her son, who was now awake and crying.

Bragg glared back at his wife and her whiny son. He decided that he needed to kill the little brat like he had the cat. The little bastard child was not his, so he had no emotional attachment to him.

Nikko pointed to a room on the left and Prescott nodded. It was the room they had been searching for. The two men ran into William Bragg's room and saw a man coming at them. Prescott fired his laser at point blank range and hit William Bragg in the chest. Guevara watched in horror as her husband was vaporized before her eyes.

She stopped in her tracks and screamed as Nikko and Prescott came into the room.

"Stop screaming or you die too," Prescott warned her.

Guevara nodded and slumped to the floor on her knees. Whoever these men were, they had murdered her husband. Why would they do such a thing, she asked herself.

The other patient in the room had also been awakened by the alarms and saw Prescott murder Bragg. The man rolled out of his bed and attacked Prescott. He was a Marine Corps officer that had been injured in a training accident that resulted in his left arm in a cast. He swung the cast at Prescott's head and connected. Prescott was knocked off of his feet and hit the floor face first. The officer turned to charge Nikko just as Nikko fired his weapon. The unfortunate young officer never stood a chance. His body turned to invisible vapor after the laser hit him in the abdomen.

Prescott stood up, shaking his head and watched as Nikko grabbed the little boy from the arms of the woman. The child was grabbing hold of Guevara's long black hair as he was being torn from her.

"No, please!" Guevara pleaded with them. "Don't hurt my son. I will do anything you ask."

Nikko smiled at her, "Get on the hospital broadcast and tell Lester Gillis that I wish to meet him in the lobby. Refuse and I kill your son."

Prescott grabbed Guevara's arm and forced her out into the hallway. She observed several hospital security guards rushing down the halls. They were all wearing red uniforms and had laser pistols in their hands. Prescott shoved Guevara to the floor and he began firing, picking off the security staff one by one. Nikko was holding the boy in one arm and firing his laser with his free left hand. Guevara watched in terror as people's bodies boiled into vapor. It was a complete slaughter by ambush. The security guards had no idea that the attack was imminent. They all died, never having a chance to use their weapons and defend themselves.

The two killers began killing doctors and nurses as they ran before them. Even the random patients that wandered out into the hallway to see what the commotion was were murdered by these heartless men. Guevara wanted to jump them, to fight back and help all of the innocents being annihilated before her. But they had her son. She could not bring herself to move out of the fear that the men would harm her son Joseph.

Soon there were no others on the floor to kill. Prescott grabbed Guevara by the arm and lifted her to her feet.

"Please, put your lasers on stun settings," Guevara pleaded with them. "You just murdered about thirty innocent people. No more killing!" She had never been exposed to such cold hearted men before. She was shaking from the fear she felt for herself and her child.

"What are you going to do about it?" Prescott laughed, sensing the terror Guevara was experiencing. Prescott knew that crowd control was most effective when the element of horror was injected into the equation.

Guevara concluded that the man enjoyed the killing as she could hear it in his voice and she saw the joy in his eyes when he pulled the trigger, ending people's lives. They had come for Gillis and Guevara deduced that it had something to do with Drayton's murder. She hoped the men would assume that the now deceased William Bragg was the father of her son. If they learned the child was the offspring of Drayton Love-Easter, they might kill him due to some twisted idea that the child would one day come after them for revenge.

"Move it!" Nikko ordered as they made their way to the stair case. Guevara saw Doctor Harding and two nurses unconscious on the floor and gingerly stepped over them. She was led down the stairs by the evil men. She silently prayed that Gillis would be bringing the cavalry with him.

Nikko was fed up with his partner, Prescott. He was a bloodthirsty assassin, reckless and unprofessional. Nikko had seen Prescott kill several innocent people on other missions. Nikko had kept his observations to himself. This time would be different as he made a mental note that he would have a long conversation with Junior Ragnarsson at the end of this mission.

As the alarms were sounding, Freya Doernitz Cardenas began ordering her staff on the upper levels to secure the patients. There was plenty of activity, as staff began attempting to calm down the patients. One nurse was in the corner of the west hallway, in a fetus position, crying. Many staff members were running here and there as the annoying alarms continued to ring.

Freya made her way to the duty desk and asked the computer to patch her through to the emergency military command. A three dimensional figure of a Marine Corps Sergeant appeared before her.

"What is the nature of the emergency?" The uniformed soldier asked.

"We have a Code Five," Freya reported to the Sergeant. "I understand that we are on Lock Down, but we have intruders. I have received security reports that there have been multiple murders on the fifth floor. Numerous unknown assailants are using lasers with patients, medical staff and security among the dead."

"We are sending a patrol now," the Sergeant assured her. "Stay away from the assailants until we arrive."

"I copy that. You don't have to tell me twice."

She read her computer screen and determined the attack was two floors below. Cardenas quickly typed in her safety codes and ordered the elevators shut down and for the bulkheads between the fifth floor, the sixth floor and her floor sealed off. She also had the computer seal the stairwell doors from level five to the ceiling shut so that no one could open them without her authorization. She was satisfied that her actions would protect the lives of the patients and staff on all of the floor levels above level five.

Before the alarms were activated, Les Gillis and Julia Steiner were sharing a cup of coffee and a late dinner in the hospital basement cafeteria. They had been friends for several years and had a lot to catch up on.

Steiner was eating a cordon bleu sandwich with a side of sliced potatoes that had been sautéed in butter and some spices. Gillis was eating a turkey sandwich on rye bread with chips. Gillis' shadow, Frank Preston, was sitting two tables away, giving the two cadets some privacy. The hospital cafeteria was large enough for fifty-three tables that could seat four persons to each table. The cafeteria line had pre-made food which would warm up in several microwave machines located along the walls. The cafeteria was busier than normal due to many of the folks on Clovis City finding shelter in the hospital due to the Sand Storm Lock Down. Gillis observed that there were only a few empty tables. At one of the tables, Gillis noticed that Tina Martinson was sitting with three other people. Martinson was in a wheel chair and hospital issued clothing as she was still a patient. She seemed to be carrying on a conversation with the others at her table.

"So Martinson made a full recovery?" Gillis asked.

"We think so. Doctor Harding is still running some tests to make sure she can medically clear her to return to the Academy. So far, there are no signs of any short term or permanent brain damage to her. She was very lucky that she is alive."

Gillis nodded, "I know Marco and Mary will be happy to know she is pulling through."

Steiner sipped from her coffee. She had put several sugar packets into her cup earlier as she loved her coffee sweet. "I heard what happened. Everyone is talking about Marco. He became the campus hero after he dared jumping out onto the surface of the Forbidden Region. The other cadets are in awe of him. Just like the old days, the Gorski Gang to the rescue. I miss the old group."

"If you miss it, then why stay away?" Gillis probed.

"Well, because I am now seeing Cormac," Steiner began and sipped from her coffee cup. "And he would most likely be upset if I started bar hopping with all of you when my ex-boyfriend is trying daily to win me back. I just feel it would not be fair to him if I did that to him."

Gillis knew that Drew Harrison was still obsessed with Steiner based on his actions over the last few months. He was always looking for Steiner and would leave her messages every day. Harrison was going through a very difficult time dealing with the end of his relationship with Steiner. Harrison lost her due to his heavy drinking. All he had to do to keep her in his life was to seek out some treatment, which he refused to do, and Steiner would still be by his side. After she left Harrison his drinking became more frequent and was causing the cadet to wake up the next day with no memory of his actions the previous night.

"You know that Cormac and I are good friends. Perhaps I could convince Cormac to join our gang. He would be a good fit. I have seen him throw down before and he can hold his own in a fight. He does listen to my advice, from time to time."

"Good luck with that!" Steiner laughed, hoping silently that Gillis would not involve Cormac in any of the Gorski Gang activities. She decided to try and change the subject from Cormac and Drew to something else. "And you, Les? Have you even tried to patch things up between you and Sophia?"

Gillis looked at his plate as he fought back the pain at the mention of her name. Sophia DuBravac was his first love and their break up was his biggest regret. On the day that Gillis received the news that the prestigious Military Intelligence Forensic Training Academy on Sikorsky's Planet had accepted him into the program, he lost DuBravac. The program was located on another planet, in a different solar system, countless Astronomical Units away from New Edinburgh. The Forensic Training Academy only accepted two hundred students each year to study for their higher degree. Gillis had been honored, thrilled beyond words, that his application had been accepted. But his joy was dashed when his girlfriend of the prior two years did not share his enthusiasm. She reacted in a way that Gillis had never imagined to be in her character. DuBravac was venomous in her words and she attacked him verbally in a way that left Gillis stunned and emotionally damaged. DuBravac, who was one year younger than Gillis, was angry that he would be gone for her senior year. She demanded that Gillis attend the lesser rated doctoral program at Clovis Academy so they could be together for her senior year. He was speechless due to her position on the matter. He did not wish to be separated from her either, but it was only for one year and that one year of time would ensure that Gillis would be eligible for promotion quicker than the average graduate starting off his career as a commissioned Lieutenant in the United Nations Space Command, as opposed to an Ensign or Lieutenant Junior Grade. DuBravac put an ultimatum on their relationship, stay with her or it was over. Gillis was stubborn and would not budge. He was going to take the opportunity to attend the better rated Academy. DuBravac's response was to walk out of his life.

"No," Gillis finally answered. "There is no talking to Sophia over the issue. She feels that my taking off for one year shows a lack of commitment to her. She knows I loved her. I love her still. But I cannot be with a woman that wants to test me and my commitment every time I turn around. It is not healthy emotionally to be put in a position of having to prove your love to someone by giving up your dreams. So, no. I have not and will not talk with Sophia regarding our dead relationship."

"You are pretty stubborn Les," Steiner told him. "Sophia now is in with my new "gang" of girls if you want to call it that. She mentions you all the time. She still loves you, Les. Please talk with her. You two were dynamite together."

Steiner was correct about that. Gillis felt complete with Sophia

DuBravac and had spent every spare moment with her. He had never felt that way for any woman before or after her. "I will give it some thought. But I know there will never be any change. I am going to Sikorsky's Planet after we graduate from here in May. Sophia will never accept that."

Steiner put her right hand on top of Gillis' left hand and held it, looking into his eyes for a moment. "Les, talk to her. I think you will find her in a more reasonable frame of mind now. She is lost without you. Just, please do not tell her I put you up to it. She would kill me if she knew I told you these things."

"I promise," Gillis assured her. "I will not say a word."

The alarms sounded in the hospital cafeteria which startled Gillis, Steiner and the other patrons. Many other hospital staff and civilians were present, eating a late meal or drinking some coffee to keep themselves awake. Gillis saw Tina Martinson in her wheel chair, looking this way and that when the alarms sounded. Her mother, father and brother, who were also present in the cafeteria, had frightened looks on their faces.

Frank Preston ran over to Gillis as two security guards on break in the cafeteria pushed themselves to their feet and ran toward the stairs.

"They're here," Preston stated the obvious. He pulled out of his jacket two spare laser pistols and handed them to Gillis and Steiner. "I assume you both know how to use these?"

"Yes," Steiner nodded and swallowed hard. Although she was studying under the science track, she had taken the introductory courses on weapons and self-defense and had excelled in the use of laser pistols. She saw the patients and their families all starting to panic. "We need to calm these people down."

Preston jumped up onto a chair and then stepped on a table top. He whistled loudly and was waving his arms at the people in the cafeteria. "Listen, for your own protection, I need you to remain here. I am an undercover MI operative. If you remain calm and stay here, you should be safe. Please do not move!"

But as was typical with humans, several of the people did not listen. They were screaming hysterically and running up the stairs. The Martinson's trusted Preston and remained where they were. Gillis and Steiner moved with Preston toward the few families that remained. Gillis got to the Martinson's.

"Tina, do you remember me? I am Les Gillis. I am one of Marco and Dominic's friends. You watched me sing at O'Malley's a few months ago. Remember?'

He watched as Tina Martinson looked into his eyes for a moment. She began to smile as if she were experiencing a personal triumph. "Yes. I remember you. You were always nice to everyone. I remember. You sang those beautiful songs with the O'Malley's and Collins family."

"Good," Gillis patted her shoulder encouragingly. He was glad for her that her memory seemed to be intact. Hopefully the trauma in her space craft crash did not cause any permanent damage. He looked to her parents and her brother, "Stay with her and do not go upstairs for any reason."

Martinson's family members nodded in agreement with his suggestion. They did not have to be told twice.

Gillis and Steiner followed Preston up the stairs. The sound of laser fire followed by people screaming and the sound of bodies falling to the floor. They made it to the lobby level and saw about thirty or more unconscious bodies lying all over. Gillis could see Guevara being held by one man, while another man was holding her son. The man holding Guevara had his laser pistol trained on her head. The two men were looking this way and that for more people to shoot. Gillis prayed that the victims were all stunned.

"Do it!" Nikko pointed his hand laser at the little boy's head and set it for a kill blast. "I will blow off his damn head. Call Gillis! Now!"

Gillis, Steiner and Preston watched as Guevara pressed the communication button on the wall. The tone of her voice was flat and emotionless as she spoke. "Les Gillis, you are requested to come immediately to the lobby and face these two men. They will kill me and my son if you do not comply. They mean what they say. They murdered Will in cold blood."

Gillis watched helplessly as Prescott slapped Guevara across her face. She screamed and fell to the floor, her left hand instinctively covering her face. Gillis began to stand up to go to them so they would leave Guevara and her child alone. Preston and Steiner held him in place by grabbing his shoulders. Steiner had seen the look that was in his eyes before which meant that Gillis was ready to fight. He had the look of a tiger ready to pounce on his prey. She was concerned that Gillis would lose his temper and charge in like a bull in a crystal shop.

"Stop it, Les. Keep your wits about you," Preston whispered into his ear. "That is what they want."

"Please do not go, Les. We need a plan of action," Steiner added.

"They killed Bragg," Gillis clenched his teeth. He had no love lost for William Bragg. Gillis found the man to be a moron and an abusive man. But murder was murder and the other victims were innocent bystanders. "All these innocent people are either dead or hurt because of me? No more, Frank. No more."

Preston nodded at Gillis, "I hear your concern and agree with you. If we are patient we can pick them off from here."

"But he has his laser trained at the child!" Steiner hissed at the two men. She recalled the day Guevara gave birth to the boy. Steiner had been present in the hospital to witness the joy of the event. They had to find a way to protect that child. "There has to be another way."

The assassin with the English accent spoke loudly as if he sensed that Gillis was nearby, "Let's start executing hostages. We have many to choose from here in the lobby."

"No, you already killed enough," Nikko responded.

Prescott was randomly pointing his laser at the unconscious bodies on the floor. "I have a shaky trigger finger, and it just might go off if Gillis does not show his mick head soon."

English and nationalistic, Gillis thought. He looked to Preston and

Steiner and winked at them, "I am going to face them. You two, stay here and wait for a clean shot."

"Les, are you crazy?" Steiner demanded.

"Maybe," Gillis whispered to her. "Maybe I am, but the bottom line is that they came for me. I can't let them kill anyone else. I never liked Bragg, but they killed him because they were after me. I have to do this. When you two get a clean shot, take it."

"Shit!" Preston said as Gillis stood and started walking toward the lobby.

"Okay, here I am you Limey bastard!" Gillis was walking slowly, his arms in the air. "You still taking orders from all of those inbred monarchs on your disease ridden island?"

"Hey, fuck you Irish!" Prescott snarled and aimed his laser pistol at Gillis. He despised anyone that spoke badly of his homeland, especially a damned rebel Irishman.

The national tensions between England and Ireland had gone back hundreds of years, even over a thousand. The Racial Wars brought back the old hatreds. Earth had been invaded by an alien race called the Akarzdamedians which caused the loss of millions of lives. The populations of Africa and the Middle East were almost wiped out by the space invaders. The aliens attempted to occupy the entire planet and rule it for themselves. But humanity fought back and eventually won. In the aftermath, many Earth leaders attempted to seize power. The feeling of jubilation at the victory was short lived. The English attempted to reestablish themselves as the world leaders and a short war erupted. Ireland led the last major offensive onto the main island of England. The English lost. But the Irish people and the rest of Europe did not treat the English as prisoners of war. They negotiated a peace treaty for all to sign, ceding the law making authority to the United Nations. Many in England had not forgotten that horrible time.

"You want me? Gillis asked as he was only a few paces from Prescott. "Come get me."

Prescott kept his laser pistol pointed at Gillis and addressed Nikko, "Let me kill him."

Nikko was growing angrier with his partner, glaring at him out of the corner of his eyes. "We take him in alive! Quit screwing around and bind him so we can get out of here!"

Prescott breathed in hard as Nikko reminded him of their mission objectives.

Gillis smiled as he observed the tension between the two men. "See? You Limeys lost all of your influence in the world because of your stupid loyalty to those Tudors and the other inbred Caligula's you followed. All of you are now nothing but a slave class to the rest of the nations. Especially to my people."

Prescott roared with rage and ran at Gillis, pulling out his knife from the sheath hanging from his hip and dropping his laser pistol. Gillis moved to his left and narrowly dodged the knife thrust. He could hear Nikko screaming for Prescott to stop.

Steiner and Preston were lying on their stomachs, trying to get a clean shot off at either Nikko or Prescott as Gillis side stepped lunge after lunge by the enraged Prescott.

Prescott was swinging his knife wildly at Gillis, cussing at him to stand still and die like a man. Gillis side stepped and leaped backwards several times to avoid the thrusts of the blade. In one swing, Gillis felt the knife tear into his sweater and cut the skin on his upper chest. It stung. Gillis gritted his teeth and kept moving to angle Prescott where Steiner or Preston could take him out. Prescott threw a kick with his left leg at Gillis. Gillis, recalling his training, stepped into the kick, blocking it with his right arm and spinning Prescott to the right. Gillis began pounding Prescott with his fists into his exposed rib cage. Prescott cried out and rolled away from Gillis as he realized he was in trouble. The cadet was a better fighter than he had thought. Prescott began crawling on the floor, desperately searching for his discarded hand laser. Sensing an opening to strike, Gillis pounced on the man and the two began rolling on the floor. Gillis had Prescott in a headlock and wrapped his legs around Prescott' squeezing him at his mid-section.

Nikko was also trying to get off a shot as well, aiming at Gillis. He fired one blast but missed as Gillis and Prescott rolled over at the last possible second. Nikko swore.

Preston nodded to Steiner when Gillis and Prescott rolled into the center of the lobby floor. Nikko was in plain view and exposed. They both aimed at Nikko and fired simultaneously. Both laser beams hit Nikko, one in the chest, the other on the leg. He collapsed to the ground as he lost consciousness. No longer encumbered by the man pointing a laser at her head, Guevara ran to her child and began to check him for any injuries.

Out of the corner of his eye, Prescott saw that his partner went down. He screamed in rage and began slashing his large knife back at Gillis. Gillis lifted his opponent up into the air, about three feet off of the floor and slammed him to the ground. Everyone present heard Prescott's scream. Gillis kicked the man over and rolled him onto his back. Gillis had inadvertently caused Prescott to fall on his own knife. The blade hilt was protruding from Prescott's chest, blood leaking onto his tunic and onto the tiled floor. Prescott was spitting blood out of his mouth, fighting for breath. He reached toward Gillis with his left arm and then died. His body went limp on the floor, his eyes staring at nothing.

Gillis turned to see Guevara and the child and was relieved that they were both unharmed. Preston and Steiner rushed to him and Steiner hugged him.

Preston made his way to Nikko and bound the man by his arms and legs with plastic twist ties. He began searching him and pulling out random forms of weaponry from the assassin's pockets and boots. He looked at Gillis with respect and concluded that he had what it takes to be a soldier.

CHAPTER ELEVEN

Yuri Gorski and Drew Harrison watched as Lund used smelling salts to awaken Chang and Quintana. After they had dragged Junior Ragnarsson back down to the fifth floor, Lund had the cadets assist in lining the three remaining killers side by side, sitting upright, with their backs against the wall. Quintana and Chang were looking at the faces of the cadets staring down at them. They saw Junior bruised and bloodied, sitting next to them. There was no sign of Montrose. Chang speculated that perhaps Montrose escaped and would possibly attack at the right moment to spring them.

Quintana noticed Gorski, one of the targets of the mission, standing before him. Gorski had a cut on his left cheek that had been cleaned and bandaged. Quintana did not see Evart or Gillis. Perhaps Montrose had captured Evart and already made his way to the escape ship. Quintana's head was pounding and he felt dehydrated, the laser blasts had that effect. He needed water and a pain killer. Quintana felt the plastic bindings on his arms and legs. He noticed that all of his weapons in his pockets were all missing. He deduced that he had been searched thoroughly. Quintana always accepted that the day would come that someone else would best him. He leaned his head back and studied the faces before him. Gorski, Harrison and the unknown man were staring back at him. Quintana wondered why this unknown cadet, that seemed to interact with Gorski and Harrison so well, had not appeared on any of the dossiers he had read in preparation for the mission.

Several other cadets were present as well, staring down at him with a wide range of expressions on their faces. Quintana speculated the new cadet that harbored so much deference from Gorski was just another face in the crowd that had not been picked up in their intelligence reports of the inner circle of friends for their target.

"Everyone is awake now," Harrison reported. His face had a few cuts that had been cleaned and bandaged.

"Good," Lund said. "You three created a huge mess. One cadet has both arms broken, three others are dead and many others have headaches similar to what you are now experiencing. Now, I decided since your man here," Lund paused and pointed at Junior, "used deadly force and killed three young men, that I would be justified to use the same force. The reason there are only three of you here now is that your fourth conspirator is dead. I killed him and I will now start killing each of you if I do not get answers."

There was a long silence. Chang and Quintana did not know if the man was lying about killing Montrose. They both kept a flat expression on their faces to avoid showing any emotion whatsoever.

Gorski was studying the men for any reaction while Lund addressed them. Their faces were rugged, toughened and emotionally withdrawn due to the years they had been in the business of killing others. These were hard men and they would not break easily.

The rest of the gang was out of the way, assisting with the care of Klaus Rhinehard and trying to contact Gillis and Staszko. Gorski had wanted his other friends to make themselves scarce to avoid any reprisals against them from the employer of the captured assassins.

Bao Mingjuan, Marco Andolini and Mary Lincoln assisted medical students Blundell and Windfohr by taking the fingerprints of the three attackers and drew their blood. The two doctoral candidates that had helped Klaus were sending the results over the holo-com Scan-Doc system to see if there was any DNA or fingerprint matches. They had also taken the photographs of the men and sent them to the United Nations criminology labs to see if there were any matches. All of these actions were done while the men were unconscious.

"They won't talk to us," Gorski concluded after staring them all down. "We should just kill them like we did the other."

Chang was considering his options. He was aware of the cyanide and liquid acid pill embedded in his molar. All he had to do was bite down hard on it and he would exit this world in seconds. He contemplated dying in such a manner. It would be quick and relatively painless. He waited to see what Junior would do.

Another cadet came running up to the three men. Ragnarsson and Quintana recognized that it was Gorski Gang member Rolf Rhinehard.

"Guys. We have Jen and Elektra on three dimensional viewer. They have information that I think you need to hear." Rolf was whispering so the three bound killers would not hear his report.

Lund whispered to Gorski, "Go talk to the women and see how they are doing. They may be able to give us something useful with these three. Rhinehard, you stay here with Drew and I."

Rolf obeyed and watched Gorski walk down the hall past several rooms and enter the Andolini room, which had become the temporary cadet war room. Jack Harcourt and Michel Evart had their room being utilized as the medical room for Klaus Rhinehard.

In the Andolini brothers dormitory room Marco, Harumi Shigeta and Jack Harcourt were gathering information from their fellow Gorski Gang members regarding the identities of the assassins. There was a life sized, three dimensional vision of Jen Staszko in the center of the room courtesy of the computer broadcasting technology. Dominic was lying on one of the beds as he was still recovering from the stun dart.

In the women's dormitory, Staszko was elated when she saw Yuri Gorski's image appear before her. "My love, you are safe," Staszko said with relief.

"Thank the Stars that you are alive," Gorski told her. "I could not stop thinking about you. Rolf said you have news."

"Yes. We were attacked, as was predicted. Marco and Mary gave me the details of your ordeal. We ambushed our would-be captors and caught them off guard. One is dead. These assassins have cyanide liquid acid capsules in their mouths. If you try and inject them with truth serum, the capsule will activate and kill them instantly. We found out the hard way. We lost one of the assassins because of the cyanide. The liquid acid in that capsule will dissolve the entire body in under a minute or two. One of our attackers will tell us everything if we afford her protection. She is terrified of one of the men that attacked you and Michel. She said his name is Dell Ragnarsson, Junior, and described him as a heartless killer. She said she is his fifth or sixth wife, he has many. The marriage was forced on her by her captors. She wants to get as far from him and the Rosenburg's as possible. We are waiting on the lawyers from the Security Council to draft the amnesty paperwork so she can give us a full sworn statement."

"That is fantastic news!" Gorski was feeling a little relieved. The last week had been an emotional roller-coaster for him and all of his friends. He needed rest and for things to return to normal. "Anything else she said that would be helpful to our interrogation over here?"

"Yes," Staszko nodded. "The woman that died here was a sister of the Ragnarsson man. Her name was Emma Ragnarsson and we have his little brother hostage also. His name is Ivar. The men you are holding will not know Emma is dead so you can bluff them. And, get this. Our cooperative witness told us that the security chief at the Baroness Hotel, that Ella Ragnarsson, remember her?"

"How could I forget?"

"She ordered this attack on us. This Ella is one mean bitch. She is a killer and she is the sister of Dell and Emma." Staszko paused for a second. "Our source, her name is Dulce. She asked if you guys would claim all of your information was coming from either Emma or Ivar."

"No problem. Anything else of use to us?"

"Not yet, my love. Once we get the amnesty agreement, she will tell us everything."

"Okay. I am going to join in on the interrogation." Gorski stood up. "I love you babe."

"Love you more," Staszko told him.

Gorski turned toward Marco, Shigeta and Harcourt, "Stay here, keep trying to raise Les. Has anyone been to his room, to check on him?

"Yes," Marco motioned with his hand. "Fenster and Frazier went to check and all they found his cat hiding under the bed. No one else was there. We have to consider the possibility that they got Les and already made it out of here."

"Okay," Gorski said, feeling horrible about that possibility. If the hired killers had gotten to Gillis then it would be virtually impossible to get him back to safety. "Keep trying to raise him."

Gorski walked briskly back down the hall way. He entered the "hostage room" and saw that the three bound mercenaries were still on the floor. Lund, Harrison and Rolf were waiting for him. Harrison had been pacing back and forth. Gorski brought the three men closer to him.

"One of these men is named Dell Ragnarsson, Junior and his sisters are Emma and Ella Ragnarsson. Emma was in on the attack on the girls' dormitory and is now dead. Ella is the security chief at the Baroness Hotel. Their little brother is named Ivar and he was also involved and Jen has him hostage. Each of our captives have cyanide capsules in their molars. I need one of you to go round up the two medical students that helped Klaus. We need to remove their teeth with the cyanide, otherwise they will commit suicide and we learn nothing. Let me do the talking."

Lund nodded and looked to Rolf, "Go get them. We will stun these three again and they can operate on them and remove the cyanide capsules."

Rolf left and began searching for cadets Windfohr and Blundell.

Gorski walked back and forth in front of the three men. "Which one of you is Dell Ragnarsson, Junior?"

The three bound mercenaries were silent. None of the three men showed any expression to betray the named individual. Gorski continued to pace back and forth as he waited for an answer to his question. He stopped in front of Ragnarsson.

"You are Junior Ragnarsson," Gorski said with confidence. He looked over the other two assassins and concluded that one was Asian and the other Latino. Ragnarsson was more of a northern European surname, so Gorski used deductive reasoning to focus on the fair skinned Anglo mercenary. Gorski had his balled fists by his side and waited for an answer. The man said nothing.

Junior Ragnarsson was startled that Gorski would know his name. That would mean that one of the other team members had sold him out. His mind was racing. Who would have talked to them, he was asking himself. He was certain that the two men sitting next to him had not talked. Was it Prescott or Nikko? Emma? Ivar? Or was it Dulce?

"I can tell that you are wondering who would give me that information," Gorski said while he was pacing once again. "Dulce, one of your team members, is dead." Gorski watched the three men for reaction to that statement. There was none.

Gorski decided to embellish, or exaggerate, as he had been taught to do in his Criminal Investigation classes. "Gillis is safe. Your hit team that was sent to apprehend him is now being held. We are interrogating them now."

Still, no observable reaction.

Junior Ragnarsson was not sure what to think. Gorski was lying, telling the truth or mixing truth with fiction. One thing was certain, Gorski knew a few names. That meant nothing or it could mean one of the team had talked. Dulce might have said her name as she died. Or, she is alive and been named by the others.

"Mister Ragnarsson," Gorski continued, "your sister Emma has told us that you have a sister named Ella on the space station." Gorski pointed to the ceiling for effect. He leaned into Junior's face and whispered into his ear. "Emma has sold you out. She is telling us everything to save the life of her little brother, Ivar."

Gorski pulled back from him. Lund and Harrison were watching the reaction of the assassin with keen interest. Lund was also certain that Gorski had correctly identified the team leader. The other two men were as of yet, unnamed. Lund was trained in the art of interrogation and felt Gorski was doing well so far. But this Ragnarsson was not going to break easily. Lund would have to jump in as the murderous 'bad cop' and get things rolling soon.

"Emma has told us that your family is knee deep in the whole cover up of the Love-Easter murder," Gorski was walking back and forth as he spoke. "Why don't you save us all some time and admit your involvement?"

Lund decided it was time for him to act. Ragnarsson was not going to talk unless he felt threatened. Lund grabbed Ragnarsson by the front of his shirt and yanked him to his feet. Gorski stepped aside. Lund slammed him against the wall. "Talk! I am ready to start killing your men and your little brother unless you cooperate!"

Junior Ragnarsson spit in Lund's face.

Lund dropped him to the floor and then walked in front of Quintana. "How about you, tough guy? Are you ready to be dropped off the roof like your friend?"

Quintana said nothing. He had suspected that Montrose had been killed, but the details were unknown to him. Dropped from a rooftop? Quintana thought that was not very original. Scary way to die, but over quickly if you landed properly. Snapped neck from the impact if you are fortunate with very little suffering. Quintana began to consider his cyanide pill. He wondered if now was the time to use it to move off this plane of existence to the next, if there was such a thing.

Quintana, like Chang, decided to follow Junior's lead. If his team leader used the cyanide option, Quintana was determined to follow the example.

Lund kicked Quintana's leg and moved his attention to Chang. Lund slapped the Asian man across the face. "Speak!"

Chang was silent, glaring back at Lund.

Gorski turned to see that Marco walking toward them. He leaned in and whispered to Gorski. "We just heard from Les. He was taken to the emergency room at the hospital. They sent two men after him. Les killed one of the men and the second is going under for surgery to remove the cyanide. Once that is done, they will pump him so full of truth serum he will have diarrhea of the mouth."

"Good news, Marco." Gorski was relieved that Gillis survived the attack on him.

"Be careful of what you let out with Drew," Marco warned. "Julia was in the middle of it all and she helped stun the second man. The two assassins killed over thirty people at the hospital. Vaporized them. Les says it is a new addition to the laser pistols that we train with at the firing range. He said it is most likely a new technological breakthrough from the scientists Rosenburg Corporation. The laser just boils the victim to a clear vapor in milliseconds. He had never seen anything like it."

"By the Gods," Gorski took in a breath. What Marco was describing was a clear advancement in laser technology and a horrible way to kill a person. "We sure have become efficient in killing each other. Any news from Jen and Elektra? Have the legal papers been finished?"

Marco shook his head, "Not yet."

"Okay, go back and let me know when it is done," Gorski told his friend.

Gorski saw that Rolf, Windfohr and Blundell were approaching. Gorski smiled and motioned for them to follow him. Gorski and Lund approached the three cadets, leaving Harrison to watch over the three hostages.

"I hear you have some dental work you need done?" Blundell asked.

"Can you do it?" Gorski asked the two medical students.

"Of course. Stun them so we can get started," Windfohr instructed. "Tooth extraction is easy. Avoiding cracking the poisonous capsule is the hard part. We need them out cold."

Without comment, Gorski and Lund pivoted around and stunned Junior and Quintana. Chang, guessing what was going to happen, bit down hard on his molar just seconds before Gorski aimed his laser pistol at him. Gorski fired too late. The cyanide was in Chang's system and the liquid acid began to absorb into his muscle and bone. All of the men watched as Chang's body began shaking and slowly dissolving into nothing before their eyes. Soon, only tiny particles of white powder remained where Chang had once lain.

"Son of a...." Harrison began.

"Lie the other two down!" Blundell instructed as he and Windfohr started pulling out instruments from their medical bags. Blundell knew that the extraction would be extremely tricky surgery. One mistake and the acid would be released. Li Mingjuan showed up with another medical case and handed it to Windfohr. The new bag had instruments that were more conducive to tooth extraction than what the two medical students had in their bags.

Jen Staszko and Elektra Papanikolaou stared impatiently at Dulce Ragnarsson as she carefully read the facsimile of the offer of amnesty from the United Nations prosecution lawyer, Sean Collins. There were three documents that Collins prepared and sent to the women's dormitory for the benefit of the witness. The second document was an agreement to enter the witness protection program and the third was a partially blank confession statement, which implicated Emma, Ivar and Ella Ragnarsson as well as Junior, Montrose, Chang, Prescott, Quintana and Nikko. The blank pages were for Dulce to fill in with hand written information.

There was a three dimensional view of Sean Collins at the side wall as he watched Dulce with his sharp eyes. Collins had received the notification from his paralegal that there was an emergency that needed his expertise. He had been relaxing at home with his family members at the time. He dropped everything and began preparing the documents that had been requested.   LaShondra Lewis and Sara Stewart took the time to explain the situation to the lawyer.   Collins quickly dictated to his computer the proper language and had his computer send the completed documents via holo-com messaging to Lewis and Stewart.

Ivar was still in the bathtub and unable to move due to the stun dart venom.

Dulce read the documents and signed all but the confession. She had agreed that she would verbally confess and give her statement before Collins, who would print it out for her to review and sign. Collins would then have Lewis and Stewart transport the woman to a secure military facility to wait until the date of her sealed Grand Jury testimony.

"State your full name," Collins directed her.

"Dulce Maria Reynolds Hernandez Ragnarsson."

"Marital status?"

"I was forced into marriage when I was only fourteen years old. I was a slave at the Rosenburg Ranch and Alfred Rosenburg sent me to marry a man named Dell Ragnarsson, Jr."

Collins spent over an hour questioning Dulce about the slave trade at the Rosenburg Ranch. She was very knowledgeable about the extent of the slave trade and which Rosenburg family members were involved. She named names, locations and dates which impressed Collins. Most witnesses could not recall such vivid details regarding several years of criminal activity.   "Please state how it was that you came to be involved in this incident," Collins requested.

The four women and Collins listened as Dulce told her story of being impressed into slavery. She and her siblings were beaten until they submitted to their new "owners," the Rosenburg family. One of her brothers resisted and was fed to some creatures before a crowd of cheering people in something called the Arena. She continued with her forced marriage to Junior Ragnarsson. She discussed her husbands' other wives and his children with them. Then she discussed her father-in-law, Dell Ragnarsson, a most cruel and efficient assassin. She told of his children that were also known killers, Junior, Emma, Ella, Erin, Ulla, Ellis, Eva and Ivar. She told them that she never personally met Ulla, Erin or Eva, but had heard their names mentioned. Ivar had never been linked to any criminal activity until this current mission. She spoke of Dark October and that Junior and Ella Ragnarsson had planned those killings. That information seemed to get more attention from Collins as he sat forward in his leather chair, listening intently.

She told them that Emma was the one responsible for planting the bomb on the Space Station Cy-7 Transport ship. Emma, like her sister Ella, would sometimes use sex to lure their victims in. But most of their killings were done with explosive devices or long range sniper technology. Dulce told them that if they searched Junior's home, they would find a large study on the second floor with stuffed human bodies of their victims and heads on plaques, hanging on the walls, like trophies. Ella had been the killers on all of those victims. There were hundreds of successful hits over the last decade that were completed by the Ragnarsson assassins.

Dulce implicated her husband in the recent political assassinations on Planet Cootron. Dulce explained how Ella took credit for killing Lieutenant Garrison on the space station.

"What about a brother named Ellis Ragnarsson?" Collins interrupted her narrative.

"I heard his name, but never met him," Dulce answered as she recalled his name. "I think he was a lawyer. I am not certain."

"And the slavery issue?" Collins wanted more information on that. Slavery had been outlawed for centuries. But, due to the many planets that the Earth Empire occupied, it had become easier for those marketing humans for sale to get away with the crime. This woman was implicating the entire Rosenburg family, the owners of the largest Territory on the planet New Edinburgh. If Collins was going to take them on in court he needed a solid case, more witnesses and physical evidence. "Tell me more on the slavery trade."

Dulce explained how she and thousands of others were living in bondage at the territory called Rosenburg's Ranch. She went into detail her memories of how her family gave her and her siblings over to the Rosenburg's. Dulce recounted the details for about an hour regarding other families she had met that were similarly situated. She gave Collins names, approximate dates, ages, descriptions and possible birth places of other slaves she knew. She pleaded with him to find her siblings.

Collins asked Dulce to continue with her story of the Ragnarsson family and their connection to the Rosenburg's. She explained how the family of her husband was the enforcement arm of the Rosenburg family. She told them of many missions that her husband and her father-in-law had participated in. There were countless murders.

Collins finally had her concentrate on the murder of Drayton Love-Easter. Dulce's eyes looked over to Elektra. "You. They were going to take turns raping you. All of them, and then they were going to slice your body to pieces. They, Caine and his friends, were going to cut you up, bone fragment by bone fragment. These people are capable of vicious and immoral acts that you could not imagine in your worst nightmares. You have no clue the horrible death you escaped that night."

Elektra felt a chill running up her spine, "Why me? Who were they?"

Dulce's eyes lit up and she tilted her head as she took in a deep breath. "You see, there is evil in this world. Evil that none of you have ever been exposed to. I have seen it with my own eyes. The Ragnarsson's are the people that go bump in the night. They are the ones that we have nightmares about as children. They stalk the innocent and cut them down. The victims never know that they are being followed and targeted for elimination. The ones that get to scream as they are killed? They are the ones that the Ragnarsson's allow to scream. Any of you ever get shivers up your back late at night? You know, when you are alone and you think someone or something might be watching you? They are. The Ragnarsson's are shadows in the dark. They come without warning and take lives. They slither away, back into the dark pits from which they came. Can any of you feel them? They probably have this conversation being recorded. They might have cameras in this room, watching our every move. The question is, will any of us live to see the sun rise? Will we? You asked me a question, Elektra. Why you? Because they can. Because they like it. Because they want to. Because you could expose them and you killed one of the children of their main employer.

"His name was Darryl Rosenburg. You succeeded in killing him that early morning on Space Station Cy-7. For that, the family will stop at nothing to see you fed to a flesh eating monster, after they take turns violating you. I hope this lawyer we are speaking with is a good and honorable man, because they will try and buy him off. All so they can get their hands on you, Elektra. In fact, I predict that by the end of the month we will all be dead anyway. They never lose. Dark October was one of their masterpieces. When the father learns of this, he will swoop in and kill us all."

Staszko put her arm around her friend for support. Elektra shivered from the way Dulce spoke to her.

"The other men involved in the attempted rape, I do not know their names," Dulce continued. "But the Rosenburg family felt it important enough to cover up the attack. Why you? I know that the group saw you either here on the planet or at the space station. They specifically targeted you and got Ella to turn off all of the security monitors at the Baroness Hotel. I know they did kill the other girl before they went to your room."

"What other girl?" Staszko cut in. "There was no other girl."

"One of your friends. She was on the third floor of the Baroness Hotel, a woman named Mejia." Dulce told them.

"April Mejia? She is our friend and she is here and very much alive," Staszko informed her. "What are you talking about?"

Dulce looked at the three dimensional Collins before her, "They were going to kill Mejia and Elektra. All I know is they killed a woman on the third floor, exactly the way I described they were going to kill Elektra. I can speculate that they killed someone else by mistake or by necessity. But a woman died that night just before they attacked Elektra and killed Love-Easter."

Collins was perplexed by this news since no body was located at the hotel during the investigation. "Who did they kill?"

Dulce shook her head, "If it was not Mejia, then I do not know. You need to arrest Ella immediately. If she catches on that you are pursuing an indictment, she will flee; change her face, her name, even her body structure. She is the most dangerous of all because she kills out in the open and she has no empathy for others. She does not hide in the shadows like her father or my husband. You also need to arrest all of the Rosenburg's for their slavery violations and illegal weapons trade. By the way, can you get me a good divorce lawyer? I want a divorce."

Collins sat back in his chair. He knew he was going to be awake all night long drafting indictments. "Lewis, Stewart, I am asking that as members of the Marines and Military Intelligence that you use your powers vested in the United Nations Code of Military Justice to arrest Ivar

Ragnarrson. Read him his rights. He is going to be charged with conspiracy, five counts of conspiracy to kidnap, attempted kidnaping of five counts, eighty-five counts of attempted assault, aiding and abetting, thirty-five counts of felony murder, and failure to report knowledge of a felony after the fact: to wit: the murder of Love-Easter and this mystery woman."

"Yes sir!" Lewis said with gusto. "For a lawyer, you are pretty cool."

"Well, thank you," Collins accepted the compliment. "Mrs. Dulce. I will personally get your marriage nullified. You were forced into the relationship and were underage at the time. You will be free of this man and his family forever and I promise that you will be protected. You will need to testify at the Grand Jury and then at trial. Once that is done, you will be given a new life and a new identity. We will send you somewhere that they will never think of looking for you."

"Thank you," Dulce said and forced herself to keep her composure. "Can you do anything for my sisters? My brother? If they are still alive?"

Collins was silent, thinking about his choice of words carefully. "I am going to do far more than just help them. When this is over, any person living as a slave on Rosenburg Ranch will be freed and all those involved will be prosecuted."

Stasko heard the determination in Collins voice and reminded her of Gorski when someone really got him angry. Lewis was right; Collins was pretty cool for a lawyer.

As the images of the cadets faded from view, Collins rubbed his chin apprehensively. He had lost his wife during the Darktober assassinations and was cognizant of the pain of losing a loved one. The killers in that event and the attack during the dust storm were similar in their viciousness. As Collins mulled over the information given to him by Dulce, he thought back to the children that had been killed during Darktober. The murders had been unnecessary, except to act as a chilling effect against any parent that might consider speaking out against the Glorious Leader. Collins considered that if he did nothing, his children would be safe, for a short time. However, in the long run, his children would be better off if the Rosenburg's could be brought to justice. The citizens would be safer without the evil family using the planet for their own selfish endeavors. The slaves that the Rosenburg family deserved freedom as well. Collins determined that he would take the risks and strike back, using the full force of the legal system. Collins would follow through with what he promised to do even though he was certain the killers would retaliate somehow somewhere. He hoped that he would be able to round up all the rats before they could circle the wagons and fight back. Collins proceeded to contact some of his top lawyers and instructed them to arrive at work early. They each had the biggest cases of their careers to prepare for.

Collins had been reporting in to Colonel Nikolai Gorski throughout the night and morning, keeping him updated as to what he was learning from the cooperative witness. The lawyer knew that he had a moral obligation to use the information to arrest all of the Ragnarsson and Rosenburg family members. His only dilemma was that the Rosenburg family was known to be members of the Royal Family. The Glorious Leader would not idly stand by while his descendants were being incarcerated and taken to trial. There would be threats, intimidation and the certain possibility of retaliation. Collins pursed his lips as he considered the possibility that if he pursued the prosecutions of the Rosenburg's that the Glorious Leader would have him arrested for treason.

Collins stood up from his black leather swivel chair and walked out of his study. His mansion had two levels underground and three floors above. Even though he was a widower, having lost two wives to the cruelty of the world, he had been able to keep all of his children relatively safe. He was the only person in the large abode that was awake. All of his children were sound asleep in their bedrooms in the upper floors. His live in nurse that helped him with his younger children was also asleep in her room.

Collins walked up the winding stair case as the winds from the dust storm began to subside. Through some of the windows, he could see the red orange hue of the morning sun illuminating the stairs and hallways. He stopped at the bedroom of one of his daughters and cracked the door open to check on her. He could see her long, dark red hair spread about over her white pillow casing as she slept. At some point in the night, she had kicked off her covers. Collins walked into the room and pulled the bed covers over her legs and torso. As he began to exit the room, she began to stir and stretched her arms over her head, yawning.

"Daddy?" Siobhan Collins called to him with a tired voice.

"Go back to sleep, baby girl."

Siobhan sat up in her bed and rubbed her eyes, "I am a senior at the Academy, daddy. I am not a baby girl anymore."

"I know," Sean Collins admitted. "I know. You grew up so fast. But in my eyes you are still my baby girl."

"Has the storm passed?"

"Yes. A new day is rising. Go back to sleep."

"You should go back to sleep, daddy. You work too much. Is everything okay?"

He nodded, "Yes, all is well. Get some rest."

"Good night daddy," Siobhan told him as he left her room, gently closing her door behind him.

Collins leaned up against the cream colored wall outside her bedroom. He wondered how he would have felt had Siobhan been in the middle of the violence that the cadets went through during the sandstorm. Siobhan had dated Yuri Gorski when she was younger. Had she not ended the relationship, it would have been plausible that she would have been in the space station with Gorski instead of Staszko. Had that been her path, then Siobhan would have been the one stalked by the assassins. The thought made Collins shudder. Siobhan was in the top five percent of her bio-chemistry and pre-med classes. She was not a fighter like Staszko or the other women that were in Gorski's Gang. Siobhan was more reserved and spent most of her spare time preparing for medical school. Getting into life or death situations on a space station or in a random bar was not her life style.

Collins felt so much pride and love for Siobhan and all of her siblings. He loved them all equally, yet differently at the same time. Each of them were growing and evolving into adults with their own distinct personalities and dreams. Collins hoped that he had instilled in each of them a strong value system to guide them throughout their lives. But even if his children were respectful of others, obeyed the law and strived to be polite and just to others, there would always be the shroud of the immoral and unjust government that denied the basic human rights that should be afforded to all. The time had come to secure a better world for Siobhan and all of the youth like her.

The world was not safe. The Glorious Leader had outlawed freedom of speech, freedom of association and ruled as a dictator. Collins was cognizant of the fact that when he filed his indictments against the Rosenburg's that young women and men would be placed in harm's way to obtain the arrests of the accused. But to not act in the face of the overwhelming evidence was immoral. He had to take on the powerful family, for the people and for his children. Collins felt that he owed it to the future generations to leave the world better off than how it was when he was born. To do that, he would have to take on the greatest challenge of his life. He would have to begin the process of taking on all of the descendants of the Glorious Leader on planet New Edinburgh. Although he had few allies to help him do what was right, he was undaunted.

Collins shook his head, "Time to shake up the eight solar systems. Time to expose the Royal Family and the Glorious Leader to all the rest of humanity. May the Gods protect us from what comes next. But I must act for my children and their future children. We cannot ignore the atrocities any longer. If a small band of cadets could do it, then so can I."

As he whispered the words to himself, the dust storm finally passed over Clovis City. The sun light was able to break through completely. A new day had arrived and if Collins was successful, a new dawn for humanity would follow.

9 781933 951713